bond Five Vagabond Five Vagabon

Klaus and Other Stories

by Allan Massie

Vagabond Voices
Sulaisiadar 'san Rudha

First published in September 2010 by
Vagabond Voices Publishing Ltd.
3 Sulaisiadar
An Rubha
Eilean Leòdhais / Isle of Lewis
Alba / Scotland HS2 0PU

ISBN 978-0-9560560-6-1

Printed and bound by Thomson Litho, East Kilbride

The publisher acknowledges subsidy towards this publication from Creative Scotland

For further information on Vagabond Voices, see the website, www.vagabondvoices.co.uk

For Charles Glass

Contents

Preface

Some three years ago in Paris, I bought the two volumes of Klaus Mann's Journals. I already knew and admired his novel *Mephisto*. It tells the story of a talented and ambitious actor who abandons his principles to become the star of the State Theatre in Nazi Berlin. The novel, with brilliant satirical portraits of Göring and Goebbels, was published in 1936, by which time Klaus had been an exile from Germany for three years. (A film of the book, directed by Istvan Szabo won the Academy Award for the best foreign film in 1981.) When I first read *Mephisto*, I knew little about Klaus, other than that he was the son of Thomas Mann, the greatest German novelist of the twentieth century. I didn't know that the actor who sells his soul to the Nazi devil in exchange for fame was based on Gustaf Gründgens, who survived his association with the Nazis, to be again the star of the Berlin theatre after the war, or that he had been Klaus's lover and also, briefly, his brother-in-law, married to Erika Mann.

The Journals do not pretend to be a work of literature. They are merely a detailed record of Klaus's daily life, high-spirited in the pre-Hitler years, despondent yet admirably resilient in the years of exile as he flitted from hotel to hotel, always working and carrying on the struggle against the Nazis, "the Brown Plague" in his words. Despite being often little more than jottings, they reveal an attractive character and offer a vivid picture of intellectual life in the Europe of the 1930s.

As the son of Thomas Mann, Klaus was a celebrity from an early age. His sister Erika, to whom he was very close, was equally famous, or, in the eyes of the Nazis, notorious. Both were richly talented, Klaus as a writer, Erika, as writer, actor and cabaret artist. Nevertheless both lived in the shadow of their father, and their precocious success provoked envy among many less fortunately situated. All his life Klaus feared he could never measure up to "the Magician", as the Mann children called Thomas.

Klaus had a gift for friendship, as Christopher Isherwood remarked in an essay after his death. Yet he was by nature depressive, also homosexual, alcoholic and addicted to drugs. His homosexuality caused him no shame, but brought him little happiness because he was attracted to men who could not return his love. He had affairs, but most of his sexual encounters were with rent-boys; he often however expresses affection for these casual partners, gratitude to them also. The alcoholism and drug-addiction were more damaging.

For a dozen years the anti-Nazi struggle gave purpose and meaning to his life. He produced magazines, made speeches, attended conferences, and travelled to the USA to try to make Americans aware of the nature of the Hitler regime and the need to engage against it. Eventually, with much difficulty, he managed to enlist in the American army, and returned to Europe in its uniform. He saw little action, being employed, sensibly, on propaganda and then working as a reporter for *Stars and Stripes*, the newspaper of the American forces in Europe. It was in this capacity that he went back to Germany in 1945 and met old family friends who had lived through the years of the regime and made what seemed to them to be necessary compromises.

All his life Klaus and Erika believed in what they called "the Other Germany". After 1945 he found it difficult to maintain his faith in its existence.

He had devoted twelve years of his life to a Cause. When its victory was achieved, he found nothing comparable to put in its place. Throughout the years of struggle he had continued to write novels and essays.

Now he found it more difficult to do so and feared that his talent had deserted him. He was dismayed to discover that neither *Mephisto* nor his autobiography, *The Turning-Point*, could be published in Germany because the resurgent Gustaf Gründgens threatened to bring a libel action if either book appeared.

Several of Klaus's friends had killed themselves during the Nazi years, and he had himself made several suicide attempts, not all half-hearted. Now, in despair, believing his talent dead and seeing no occasion for hope, he succeeded in killing himself in Cannes on the 21st of May, 1949. He was only forty-two

Reading his Journals, I found myself drawn to Klaus, even obsessed by him. For a writer there is only one way to be rid of such an obsession.

I knew from the first this would be a novella dealing with his last days in the miserable wet spring of 1949. It would run, I thought, to 30,000 words, a difficult length to publish, but I wanted something long enough to say what I wanted to say, short enough to be read in one sitting.

Some of it draws on Klaus's own writings, freely adapted. Such are the scenes in which he remembers his post-war return to Germany and his conversations with André Gide, whom he regarded as his mentor. Other scenes are of my own invention, as I imagined his last days may have been. The invented scenes include a lunch with Somerset Maugham at the Villa Mauresque. Klaus knew and liked Maugham, but I have no reason to think such a lunch took place then.

In his last weeks, Klaus was trying to write a novel, to be called *The Last Day*. According to Andrea Weiss, author of *In the Shadow of the Magic Mountain: The Erika and Klaus Mann Story*, it "was conceived as two parallel plots, one concerning a cosmopolitan New Yorker, named Julian Butler..., the other concerning a writer in East

Berlin named Albert Fuchs.... Only a few pages exist from this unfinished novel."

I haven't read them, and the passages of the novel, embedded in my narrative, are my own invention.

I am indebted to Andrea Weiss for her sympathetic study of Klaus and Erika, and have also drawn on Hermann Kurtzke's excellent biography of Thomas Mann. The table (pp. 61-62) listing the qualities or attributes of homoeroticism and married love is Thomas Mann's, from his essay "On Marriage", originally entitled "Marriage in Transition".

§

Like many novelists I began by writing novels which were not finished and by publishing short stories. Two of these early stories appear here, the final ones in this collection. I was very lucky. Both were first published in *The London Magazine*, then edited by Alan Ross. It was arguably the best literary magazine of its time, and so I felt I had started at the top. I owe a lot to Alan Ross, as do other novelists he published such as William Boyd and Graham Swift. Ross was a man of many parts: naval officer on northern convoys during the war, poet, essayist, auto-biographer, cricket correspondent for *The Observer*, and racehorse owner. He was an ideal editor, not least because he replied to submissions quickly and sympathetically. If he refused a piece, he told you why and his advice was good. Rejecting one story, he told me to fine myself for any echo of Hemingway. His approval and acceptance of stories gave me confidence I needed. Nothing is more important to a writer at the beginning of his career than being published in good company. This is why literary magazines are important, even when their readership may be small.

When you are in the habit of writing short stories, ideas for other ones present themselves. I recently came on a notebook with a list of such. Some of the stories were written and published, but are either now lost or not worth republishing. Others were never written, and reading the list, I know I could not recapture the mood in which they had been conceived.

Later, when I managed to finish a novel and have it published, and then wrote other novels, ideas for short stories dried up. I don't know why. A few were written in response to occasional requests, and some of these are published again here. "Train Talk" originally appeared in *The Fiction Magazine*, edited by Judy Cooke; it was a good but short-lived publication. "Poor Toni" was commissioned by The Daily Telegraph, and "Bertram's Funeral" by the BBC. Both subsequently appeared in anthologies. The oddest of these commissions came from the Tate Gallery Magazine. It was devoting an issue to Turner and, perhaps because I had recently written a book called *Byron's Travels*, I was asked to write a story about a possible meeting of Turner and Byron in Venice. The result is "Venetian Whispers". I was never convinced it was a success, but I rather like it.

More recently I have started writing short stories again. "Forbes at the Festival" was published in Standpoint magazine, "Sheila and Ronnie" in The Scottish Review of Books.

I hope there will be more stories, but one can never be sure.

Klaus

Klaus

I

Klaus woke from a dream of the house in Poschingerstrasse when they were young and happy. He was again the child in the sailor suit and Erika was with him dressed as the Princess she had always been in his eyes.

Late morning sunlight slid through the green shutters and lay on the sleeping face of the boy beside him. He ran his finger along the line of the jaw on which there was only a soft down rather than stubble. He let it lie on the boy's lips and heard a little sigh, and leaned over and kissed him with gratitude rather than desire. There was aniseed on the breath. The boy from the Zanzi Bar gave a soft moan and his hand came up from under the duvet and rested on Klaus's.

For a moment life was as you hope it is and sometimes, just sometimes, believe it may be. As it had been when they lived in that house in Munich and were young geniuses together.

All gone, swept away by time's flooding river.

The reality was the house as he had seen it for the first time in more than twelve years and the last time ever, in May 1945. He found the roof and most of the interior walls gone, result of an Allied bomb in September '42. The sight left him hollow as the building. You can't go back.

A girl was watching him from an empty window on the second floor, his window, his old bedroom. She looked at him without sign of curiosity or fear, and he called out to her in his discarded native tongue.

"Come up," she said, indicating the means by which he might do so, a rickety ladder propped against the wall.

Who was she? What was she doing there? Did she know whose house this had been?

"Does it matter?" she said. "None of that matters now."

But he persisted.

"Some writer, they say, who didn't get along with the Nazis. So they confiscated it, like they stole anything they fancied, and put it to their own use."

"As what?" he said.

"It was the SS took it over. They established a *Lebensborn* here."

"A *Lebensborn*?"

He wasn't sure he had got it right and not only because he had difficulty in following her accent, which wasn't Bavarian but from somewhere north or east, Saxony perhaps. But if he had, the word was new to him. Even the language he had been born in had changed.

"What do you mean?"

"You don't know anything, do you, even though you're the first American soldier I've met who speaks German."

Was there contempt or pity in her voice as she stood bare-legged in a shapeless grey woollen dress stained with all manner of substances?

"A *Lebensborn*," she said again, "where they bred proper little Nazis, specimens of the true Aryan race, the future of Germany. Hadn't you heard?"

In his own bedroom perhaps.

"And you?" he said, "were you...?"

He didn't know how to put it, without offence. But she smiled for the first time.

"Not me. Look at me."

She was small and dark, and thin as only the starving and malnourished are thin.

"And you're living here now?" he said.

"Why not? I've nowhere else. Not that I'm the only one, though there's some as says it's too dangerous, that the whole building'll fall in. So what if it does, that's what I say."

"How old are you?"

"Sixteen, seventeen, I forget."

"And your parents?"

"God knows. I don't. I haven't seen them since '43. Do you want me?"

She made the offer in a flat voice, take me or leave me, without expression, without either hope or repugnance. He shook his head, but gave her money, American dollars.

You can't go home. You can't go home anymore.

The boy shifted position, his hand now resting on Klaus's belly.

To be able to sleep like that.

You can't go home anymore. Klaus had known it for a long time now.

Except in dreams and memories.

Of Erika when nothing and no one had come between them, in the days when they were taken for twins and acted as twins and thought of themselves and each other as twins.

Evenings in the drawing-room, the heavy dark crimson velvet curtains drawn, the whole family assembled, himself and Erika holding hands on the Biedermeier sofa, smoke blue-grey from the Magician's Maria Mancini as he read to them from work-in-progress, novels, stories, essays, addresses to be given to learned societies, occasionally what Klaus later recognised as polemics. And they listened, all of them, even Golo who distrusted the Magician, in respectful and obedient silence, even the youngest who must often have understood nothing.

He was working now, Erika had said in her last letter, on *Felix Krull, Confidence Man*, the comic novel he had set aside, unfinished, perhaps scarcely begun, half a lifetime ago.

"There are bits of you in it now, and Felix is as beautiful as you were as a boy."

Letters – so many to write, so many lying unanswered, so many he had sent off asking, begging, for work, the work that would give him, for the time being, reason to go on, and which still awaited a reply.

The sunlight had died away. It was raining now. Grey light. They said they couldn't recall such a miserable spring here in Cannes.

That morning – how old was he? thirteen? fourteen? – when the Magician had entered the bathroom as he lay in the water with a little cloud rising between his legs. and had stood there smoking and gazing, placidly and yet with an intensity that made Klaus blush, until, remarking only, "You really should bolt the door, dear boy," he turned away.

There had been two other visits, two other encounters, on that return to what had been his homeland.

In both cases Klaus wanted to know, simply to know, how men he had admired had contrived to remain there and endure, live through, the years of the regime.

First, Emil Jannings, the actor who had so movingly depicted the disintegration of a once proud and respected personality in the film of *The Blue Angel*, made from Uncle Heinrich's novel, *Professor Unrat*.

Old Emil, smiling family friend, received him in his beautiful house on the Lake of St Wolfgang, near Salzburg, and was delighted to see him

"Dear boy, your arrival brings the promise of the return of spring."

His sweet and charming wife Gussy enfolded Klaus in an embrace. Gussy, previously married to Conrad Veidt, anti-Nazi, refugee, who had flourished in Hollywood – playing Nazis, notably Major Strasser in *Casablanca*.

Nevertheless, "Look, Emil," Klaus had said, "I must tell you I am here, not as a friend, but as a reporter for the US army newspaper, *Stars and Stripes*, and I want your story for it. That's all. I don't care," he lied, "if you were a Nazi or not. I just want to be able to tell what it was like for a distinguished actor to live through these years."

"Me a Nazi?" Jannings had laughed, and called on Gussy to bring a bottle of Moselle – "the best we have, schatz," he said, smiling and extending his arms wide as if he too wanted to fold Klaus in them.

"Oh," he said, "what happy memories return, dear boy, when I see you again! What fun we had in the old days! Do you remember that Christmas Eve in Hollywood – when was it? 1930? – when you and Erika descended on us like visiting angels, or babes in the wood, perhaps? And that delightful carnival in Munich? Seeing you again, dear boy, obliterates, quite wipes out, cxpunges, the memory of the grim years we have endured. Endured and suffered, for don't think that because you scc us here in our beautiful home, we have escaped suffering. And your father? He is well, I trust, and about to return to Germany now it's all over? And your dear uncle Heinrich? What a part he wrote for me ! Ah, my dear, pour the wine. You won't have drunk wine like this in America. Me a Nazi? Of course not. I'm an artist, a mere actor, a man without politics. It's true I appeared, as you may have heard – appeared as the star of course – in that film, which you might call propaganda – *Ohm Krüger* – a good part and I made the most of it – but only because I had no choice. I was compelled to. Dr Goebbels – dreadful little man – blackmailed me. It would have been suicide to say 'no'. You will remember that I had a Jewish grandmother..."

And so it went on. All the old charm was there. Briefly Klaus succumbed, set scepticism aside, and the piece he wrote was, well, generous. Emil, he suggested, had gone as far in resistance – or what had become known as "internal exile" – as he dared without endangering his life, his family, his career, or even his bank account.

Then the letters came, indignant, unanswerable. Jannings, they said, had crept and crawled like the worst and most contemptible of scoundrels. One correspondent sent Klaus a biography of old Kruger with an introduction by Emil in which he lavished praise on Goebbels, thanking him in the most servile fashion for giving him the opportunity to play the great part of the Boer leader who had defied the might of the British Empire.

Shameful.

And Klaus thought of how the old fellow had laughed and smiled and lavished endearments on him as he insisted they had another bottle of "this golden wine"...

Yet now, looking at the sleeping boy beside him, he found himself saying – actually speaking the words aloud as people do who live mostly alone – "Poor old Emil – he wanted to stay alive in his beautiful house drinking good wine and would submit to any degradation that allowed him to do so..."

He turned to the little table by the bed, picked up his notebook and a pencil, and scribbled: "There is no end to the humiliation people will accept. So Emil divested himself of all responsibility for anything but his own comfort, and will doubtless continue to live at ease with his dishonour. But, as for me, if I was to tell my own story, would it be more edifying? Certainly I can claim consistent resistance to the Brown Plague, but how effective was anything I did? And what's my life been? The story of an intellectual who never found the community he was searching for, who lived disconnected, rootless, a solitary wanderer – a German who wanted to be a European – a European who wanted to be a citizen of the world – an individual hopelessly opposed to the spirit of the age he was condemned to live in – and who, now when victory has been attained, finds its fruit bitter, and himself alone…"

"What are you writing?"

The boy leaned on his shoulder.

"Words, words, nothing but words."

"Can we get some coffee sent up?"

"Of course."

"Is that what you do for a living? Just write?"

"It's what I am."

It's what I was.

His other visit had been to Richard Strauss who wasn't, as Emil had been, a family friend, though of course the Magician knew him as he knew every artist of note. This time Klaus didn't give his name. He was simply the American reporter.

Strauss was eager to speak. He was both complacent, sure of his status as the foremost composer of the age, and indignant. It was good that the Nazis had gone. As for Hitler, "he never appreciated my work. With him it was Wagner, always Wagner. Would you believe it? He almost never attended a performance of any of my operas…"

There had been one exception: Hans Franck, the Governor-General of Poland. "Now he had a proper appreciation of my work. A man of taste and culture…"

Organiser of the death-camps.

"What a strange country this was," Klaus had written, "one where even the creative artists, even those touched with genius, had forgotten the language of humanity. There was, I discovered, an abyss separating me from those who had been my countrymen."

That had been more than five years ago. Since then he had struggled to find a new purpose to give meaning to life.

The boy put down his coffee cup.

"Time I was on the boat," he said.

He got out of bed, stood a moment naked, admiring himself before the glass – innocently? – yes, why not innocently?- pulled on his trousers and singlet, ran his hand over his dark curly hair.

"Pass me my jacket," Klaus said.

He took a couple of notes from his wallet and handed them to the boy.

"You're all right, Klaus."

"You think so? Sweet of you."

"Sure. You like me too? Another time, yes? Not to-night, because I'll be with my girl. But the day after? At the Zanzi? OK?"

He bent down and kissed Klaus on the cheek.

"Yes, you're all right," he said again.

The door shut behind him. Klaus listened to his steps descending the stair.

If only I was. He got out of bed, wrapped a towel round his waist,, stood at the window and watched the boy till he was out of sight. Then he filled a syringe with morphine and injected.

II

Humiliation, he had known that for a long time. The humiliation of addiction, the humiliation of failure, the humiliation of dependence. Once in New York, when he was editing *Decision*, his most ambitious magazine, he had overheard Auden's lover Chester dismiss him as "the superfluous Klaus". And there were those who mocked him for making the journey through life clinging to the Magician's coat-tails and seeking to bask in reflected glory.

The humiliation of lovelessness, the knowledge that he could never find what he sought because those to whom he was most attracted could not respond in kind. The boy from the Zanzi bar, Miki, the latest – perhaps the last – in a line that stretched out and out and out would lie making real love with his girl tonight, and, if he returned to Klaus and made a show of affection which nevertheless might not *au fond* be entirely false and not entirely mercenary, there would nevertheless be condescension in his tender embraces. It hadn't always been like that, but it had been like that for too long and far more often than not.

He slipped on a dressing-gown and settled himself at the table wedged in the corner of the room. It was ill-balanced and he took a newspaper and shoved it under one of the legs. At how many such tables had he sat in the thousand and more hotel rooms that had been his home since he had no home?

Yesterday he had managed only some hundred and fifty words and had brought his character Julian to the point at which he contemplated death. Well, there was nothing false there. Klaus had known the temptation of that abyss too well for too long not to tell it truly, and yet, though the emotion was real, the words themselves were leaden.

If you can't go home anymore, perhaps what kept you going, writing, was now being taken away from you? His muscles were wasted. Perhaps his mind and imagination also?

He thought of the Magician who denied himself so much in the name of Art. But Klaus knew himself to be an artist who had never managed to believe that Art must take precedence over all else. Which was perhaps why... he leafed through the pages of his novel which stank of mortality.

There were letters to write. There were always letters to write, and now, as for so long, too many of them were begging, for work, for money, for reputation, for some token of regard.

His Julian was a New Yorker, a man of charm, substance, sensibility, who had been what they called a "premature anti-Fascist" and was therefore viewed as suspect by the FBI; he has now come to believe that America, once truly "the best last hope of mankind", was being transformed, little by little but inexorably, into a police state. His story marched with that of Albert, novelist and playwright in East Berlin, who, living with Communism, despairs and renounces his membership of the Party, for which he had suffered in the camps.

But the narratives did not march. That was the problem. It was as if Julian and Albert both found their feet stuck in a muddy swamp.

He envisaged their predicament clearly. But what should they do? What words should they speak? Were there any words that could evoke their utter numbness?

Scene in a café in East Berlin. (Name the street, Klaus, he noted.) Albert is with his friend Moritz. They haven't seen each other for a dozen years, not since Moritz got out, to the Soviet Union.

"And you still believe?" Albert says.

Someone had told him that Moritz spent three years in one of Stalin's camps. Subject for an essay, he thinks: compare and contrast Nazi and Bolshevik discipline of deviants and dissenters.

"But I was neither," Moritz would say, "and yes, of course, I still believe."

Was that possible? More to the point, could he, as novelist, make it plausible?

"Some early Christian," he wrote – but who? Check – "said 'Credo quia impossibile.' I believe though it is impossible." Moritz was in danger of seeming more credible than Albert who had come to believe in nothing, since what he wanted to believe in seemed more impossible than belief in a God in the sky. Or, it goes without saying, in the Kremlin.

Perhaps they might – Albert and Moritz – be playing chess?

"You win, my friend, because you do not care if you lose."

Someone had said that to him once – where? when? who?

Klaus got to his feet, slowly and awkwardly. He was sweating again and there were stabbing pains in his calves.

He lay down on the bed. The smell of the boy lingered there, faintly. It would soon be gone. He drifted into sleep to the sound of the rain pattering on the balcony.

It was no more than a half-sleep in which he found himself lost in a labyrinth and trying vainly to push his way through the thick box hedges. When he woke he was sweating freely. Dream or drug?

To the post office. Three letters of no importance; no money. Impossible to eat lunch. An afternoon to kill. And still this rain, certainly less awful than his mental and physical state, yet perhaps contributing to it. How to survive? Cinema, no matter how stupid and depressing the movie. But still light when he emerged. What to do? Impossible to return to the loneliness of the hotel room.

He sat at a café table, ordered a whisky-soda, took out a notebook, and glanced through it. Jottings for an article on "The Ordeal of the Post-War Intellectual". Oh là là.

III

He was melancholy by nature, had always been, despite moments of gaiety, depressive. The drugs of course, but which came first? Cause and effect, effect and cause? Without them, and alcohol, so often life would have been impossible. He understood his own condition, but understanding pointed to no cure.

Of course there had been times of happiness, ecstatic, excited happiness. Hamburg, for example. There were four of them: Erika naturally, Pamela, Gustaf and himself. They were so very young, though Gustaf was half a dozen years older; nevertheless in his single-minded ambition, innocent in those days, often seemed the child among them. A controlling and brilliant child, unspeakably precocious – and ignorant at the same time. A bizarre and irresistible combination. They were all in love with each other, though later it seemed Gustaf had really been in love with himself alone. Love-hate, for he was burnt up by bitterness and resentment, and all because he had been deprived by birth and upbringing of the world that belonged to the other three by inheritance. Klaus could never forget his first appearance – his irruption into their hotel room like a neurotic messenger of the gods, dressed in flapping leather overcoat, sandals on his feet, a monocle in his eye, his voice rising and soaring like birdsong.

"Your play," he shrieked, "marvellous, or will be when I have taken it in hand. I insist I must produce it, with all four of us in the cast..."

They were overwhelmed. Klaus, utterly dazzled, fell in love with him on the spot. He wasn't beautiful, except when he chose to be, as Hamlet for instance or a young man in a Wilde comedy. Other times ugly, in Strindberg wickedly ugly. Indeed he could be whatever he wanted.

He was all talent, no substance. Klaus adored him for weeks, even months.

He called to the waiter for another whisky-soda and lit a cigarette, Lucky Strike, because the name had always appealed to his sense of irony…

Anja and Esther, a play about – what else? – a group of young people in love with each other and in the manner of the post-war generation despairing of their parents, against whom their rebellion was – he now admitted – a thing only of words and gestures. For of course, in the case of Klaus and Erika, there was in truth little to rebel against. The Magician and Mielein let them go their own way, the one with a tolerant and superior irony – but irony is always superior, isn't it? – the other with unquestioning love. And Pamela, in thrall to her dead father, the famous playwright and at ease with her soft and comfortable mother, Tilly, had no cause for revolt either. And yet they felt rebellious. The spirit of the age, or at least the decade. Was it merely an expression of this need that made Erika and Pamela lovers, and had nevertheless led Klaus to engage himself to Pamela? Though they had never slept together; he had never slept with a woman. To do so would have been a betrayal of Erika…

As for Gustaf, the glittering and shabby prince of the theatre, who on stage could be whatever he chose, and always convincingly, he adored his mother, married to a failed shopkeeper who had taken to drink, and was also ashamed of her. What embarrassment her expressions of love, faith and confidence in his genius caused him! And how he needed them too!

In bed Gustaf was now dominant, now abject. "How you must despise me, Klaus!" he moaned. "How I despise myself!" Then, at another moment, he was all ferocity, wrestling with Klaus, forcing himself upon him, commanding him to submit. Or suddenly tender, "oh, my

Klauschen, you are my salvation. Never have I loved anyone as I love you, for you alone understand me..." And he would let his hands, with their reddish hair like pig's bristles, wander over Klaus's willing body. There were moments too when Klaus found him repulsive, for, while Gustaf could make himself elegant on stage, in the bedroom, naked, you couldn't deny that his thighs were flabby and his bottom too big. Yet for weeks none of this mattered, though now the memory was disgusting. That, however, was on account of what happened some time later.

Not certainly the fact that suddenly he proposed to Erika, she accepted him, and they were married. That was bizarre, even if for her it was in part an experiment and in part a means of belonging even more completely to Klaus. To marry his lover, just as her lover had become her brother's fiancée... It made perfect sense, to the quartet, if not to the world. Or perhaps not. He couldn't be sure, even now, what made sense to Gustaf.

As for the parents, well, they behaved, as always, in character. The Magician smiled and bestowed his blessing. The marriage was absurd, certainly, but the absurd must be accepted. When he wrote to Erika on her honeymoon he sent his warmest wishes to her dear friend, Pamela, not her husband. Mielein merely offered the sensible judgement that she had never considered her eldest daughter to be "the marrying kind".

And the wedding itself was a comedy of manners, not least because the bride's uncle, Mielein's brother, the older, original Klauschen, couldn't refrain from flirting with the groom, who, to mark the occasion, had made himself handsome, the way a Wagnerian tenor should be handsome.

It couldn't last, if only because there was when you came to think about it no good reason for the marriage to have taken place, since it wasn't to the taste of either of the "happy couple". But what sealed its fate, and at the same time separated Gustaf from the trio, was that newspaper photograph with the caption: "Children of Famous Poets staging a big show in Hamburg". It should have been all right, even pleasing, for the original photograph featured the four of them, but a Berlin paper, whose picture editor concluded that no one in the capital had ever heard of Gustaf Gründgens, which was then admittedly the case, cut him out, leaving Klaus there framed by Erika and Pamela.

When he discovered the embarrassment, which to his tender self-esteem was a cruel insult, he sat silent, lips closed, but an expression of agonised anger and resentment on his face. And Klaus made the mistake, the cruel mistake, of trying to turn it into a joke, inviting laughter rather than expressing sympathy or, better, indignation on behalf of his insulted lover. Later he concluded that Gustaf had never forgiven him for this.

In those days Gustaf proclaimed himself a Communist, though he had never read any Marxist literature, and talked of launching a "Revolutionary Theatre" in Hamburg. He inveighed against the rich and the bourgeoisie, even at the family dinner table in Munich.

"But it is natural you should feel like that, my dear son-in-law," the Magician said, and Gustaf, whose antennae were so acute, read contempt in the apparently friendly words. That was the trouble. He quivered with sensitivity, but like many who are abnormally thin-skinned, alert to any appearance of a slight, would speak harshly and cruelly in complete disregard of his listeners' feelings. The world existed for him and him alone; the globe spun round him.

Another whisky? Why not? If he got a little drunk, he might not need another dose of the drug that evening.

"Hey there, Klaus," a voice called, and, looking up, he saw Miki, the boy from the Zanzi bar, with his arm round his girl. He leaned over and kissed Klaus, and insisted his girl did so too.

"This is Annie," he said. "Annie, meet my mate Klaus."

Annie was pretty with dyed blonde hair. She looked about sixteen.

"Buy us a drink, Klaus. I've had a hard day. Annie, you won't believe how much this guy knows, it's sensational. Have you been writing, Klaus? If it's a story, tell it us, Annie loves stories."

"I'm sorry," Klaus said, "it's only an essay. Very boring."

"We're going to the boxing. Why not come with us? It's an amateur show. One of my mates is fighting and, believe me, he'll need all the support he can get."

The waiter brought them drinks: another whisky for Klaus, a pastis for Miki and a lemonade for Annie, who put her arm round her boy and whispered in his ear.

"That's all right," Miki said, "Klaus is a good guy, I tell you."

What had she said? What doubts or disagreement aired?

Miki laughed and hugged her. Klaus, warmed by his presence, envying, however absurdly, Annie, thought, the boxing. Why not? It would fill an hour or two.

"Let's go then," Miki said.

IV

Sleep evading him, he turned as so often to that afternoon in the Carlton Tea Rooms in Munich, springtime 1932. He had gone there only because the Café Luitpold across the street, which he preferred, was full of SA men, and so it was surprising to find Hitler in the tea room with some of his – what could you call them? – not colleagues, surely – henchmen, disciples? Strange to find that the Nazi leader had seemingly chosen not to be surrounded by his Brownshirt thugs.

For a moment Klaus had come close to walking out. Then he thought: no, this is interesting, a chance to observe the man from close quarters.

The Fuehrer was eating strawberry tarts, stuffing them into his mouth one after the other. (Klaus too was fond of these tarts – the pastries at the Carlton were exceptionally good – but it would be years before he could enjoy one again.)

What struck him was not only Hitler's greed, but his insignificance. He was right about the greed – the man looked, as he later wrote, like "a gluttonous rat" – and that greed would be satisfied by nothing – it was all-consuming. But as for the insignificance which led Klaus to write that this flabby and foul little man with no marks of greatness would never come to power, well, that alas was a different story... "You're a failure", he had thought, "a grubby little failure..."

He was close enough to overhear some of the conversation, which to his surprise was about the theatre and the actress Therese Giehse, who was a friend of both Klaus and Erika, but especially Erika.

"She's very talented," someone said, "but you must know that she is Jewish, Not altogether Jewish, I admit, but there's a bit of the Jew in her..."

"That's absurd," Hitler said, "just nasty gossip. Do you suppose I can't tell the difference between a filthy Jewish clown and a great German artist."

Well, you're a fool then, Klaus thought happily, a pretentious and absurd idiot, for Therese would have laughed to hear him. She was proud to be purely Jewish.

Yes, he could still laugh at Hitler then. He could even decide that Hitler looked just like a notorious serial killer called Haarmann who invited a succession of street-boys to his apartment in Hanover from which they never emerged alive. It was a good private joke to compare Hitler to Haarmann, but now he thought: I got that right anyway, serial killer par excellence, even if his own nasty little paws were never soiled with his victims' blood. Millions of victims and the dictator's paws smelling only of eau de cologne!

And the Germans, his own people as he had reluctantly to acknowledge, were they accomplices or, as many of them believed in the desolation of the war-ruined Reich, his first victims? They were both, of course, and many of them willing victims of his lies as well as eager accomplices in the horrors he decreed. You couldn't get away from that. Klaus – and Erika – had dreamed and written of "the Other Germany", their Germany, a land of artists and intellectuals, of professors and lawyers, engineers and honest businessmen, decent workers and peasants, a civilised country, which may never have existed, or if it had – and surely they weren't entirely wrong? – had surrendered its judgement, its intellect, its soul, to a raving monster preaching hate and destruction.

He had never understood how this could be, but he knew that he had both overestimated and underestimated the people from whom he sprang.

And some who should have belonged to "the Other Germany" had been among the first to betray it.

He thought for instance of his friend, the novelist W. E. Suskind, a charming man who was in the habit of writing delightful stories about the girls he fell in love with. Suskind had stayed in Germany, even written to Klaus in his first or second year of exile entreating him to return. Have you gone off your head? Suskind had asked, become some sort of republican fanatic? Why don't you look at what is actually happening here in Germany rather than listening to our enemies' propaganda? Life under Hitler is enchanting and exciting. Do you think that I would still be here if it was dishonourable to remain in Germany? Can't you trust me and trust my judgement?

Trust him? He felt sorry for him when he learned that he had agreed to become editor of a literary magazine, sponsored and financed by Dr Goebbels...

Or there was Willi. He turned over in bed as he thought of Willi, whom he had picked up one afternoon in the Tiergarten: a blond open-faced boy with a slightly snub nose, well-muscled, "swimmer's build" as they said in advertisements. His father had been killed at Verdun and Willi was an only child. He did some casual labouring and was happy to rent himself out. "My mother's got this cough," he would say, "I think it's consumption..." It always worked. He grinned when he said that. On the other hand it happened to be true. They had good times together, not only in bed where Willi was eager and uncomplicated, romping like a puppy. They were fond of each other and Willi never minded Klaus's teasing which was, as a matter of fact, rather cruel, playing on the boy's ignorance. "So what?" Willi would say when Klaus told him some monstrously fanciful false fact. "Doesn't matter to me." He liked Klaus enough to introduce him to his mother, who also took to him. "You've got a good friend there, Willi," she said. "See you don't lose him with your nonsense." Klaus liked her too, had no illusions she didn't understand the relationship between him and her adored but irritating son, didn't know very well what they got up to together. Klaus took him on trips, to the seaside for instance and not only because Willi looked marvellously sexy in his bathing-costume. As Klaus lay back, head on a rolled towel, and watched his boy stride up the beach, he thought of the Magician's old Aschenbach and the Polish lad in Venice and knew he had the better of it. Once when he was in Paris, Willi, on a whim, only minutes after receiving a postcard from him, took the night-train, sitting up in third class, burst into his hotel room, flung himself on him, and covered his face with kisses. Klaus felt his sex stir at the memory, so many years old.

Willi had possessed, despite the life he led, the freshness of innocence. Klaus thought him safe from the vile intoxicating rhetoric that poisoned the air of Germany. Then one day, when he had returned to Berlin after a few weeks or months away, he encountered him in the Alexanderplatz wearing the black uniform of the SS.

"What's come over you?" he said, "why are you wearing these monkey clothes?"

He was shocked and partly, he had to confess, because in that uniform Willi looked more beautiful, more attractive, more enticingly sexy than ever.

For a moment a shadow of what might have been embarrassment crossed the boy's face.

"So what? " he said. "So what? It's not for the fun of it, but a guy has to live..."

"But not like that," Klaus said. "You know I'm always..."

"Ready to rent me?"

"That's not what I meant. You know that."

"OK, I know that. But so what? You're not going to be about for ever, are you, and besides what's good enough for millions of Germans is good enough for me. We're going to be the bosses, Klaus."

"You, Willi, a boss? I don't think so. Do you believe in all that nonsense the Nazis spout? Do you really believe it?"

Willi smiled, the same sweet smile he had always smiled.

"So what if I don't believe it?" he said. "Who does, anyway? I don't give a damn. Who cares what I believe or don't believe? It doesn't matter, Klaus. You're clever, you should know that. But they're going to be the bosses, and that's all there is to it. You're either for them or they're against you. Besides, it's not what you think. There are lots of chaps like me in the SS, good guys, fun. You don't understand, Klaus, clever as you are. I'm a German and this is what Germany is going to be. Isn't that clear enough?"

"Oh yes," Klaus had said, "it's clear, horribly clear."

He was about to turn away, when Willi touched him on the arm and said,

"Don't be mad at me, we've had good times together, and I'm still fond of you. Look after yourself, and if you ever find you need a friend in the Party, well, you know where to reach me..."

Where to reach him...

Where indeed? In a mass grave at Stalingrad perhaps? And what crimes would that once happy and innocent boy have committed, even willingly? And if by chance he had survived, what memories would assail him?

Klaus got out of bed, poured two inches of whisky into a smeared glass, took a sleeping pill, and, waiting for it to work, sat by the window looking out on the wet street and a weeping sky.

V

He had always been happier in France than anywhere, which was why he was now in Cannes, where however he was miserable and knew that the tether which held him to life was fraying. He borrowed an umbrella from the hotel proprietor and with the rain splashing the bottom of his trousers made his way to the station to enquire about trains to Paris. For Paris, throughout his wandering years, was the city to which he always returned: Hôtel Jacob, Hôtel Le Royal, Hôtel des Saints-Pères, Hôtel Chambord, Hôtel Madison, Hôtel St-André, Hôtel Pont-Royal, Hôtel Recamier, Hôtel d'Alsace, Hôtel je-ne-sais-quoi...

But he did no more than enquire. His Paris was pre-war. Now, on his last visit, he had been conscious of a sourness in the air. Hard to account for. Those who had been in the real Resistance were disappointed. There had been no renewal. The Fourth Republic was turning out to be as petty and corrupt as the Third. Then there were the ghosts of Vichy, some of whom had been his friends, anti-Fascists in the last years of what had passed for peace, who had nevertheless accepted the reality of the debacle of 1940 and turned to the aged Marshal, whom Klaus had thought "as hideous as Hindenburg", perhaps even more dangerous, and the promise of a National Revolution, turned in a mixture of nervous fear and wary hope. Which was of course disappointed. And there were others, among them also men and women he had liked, who had collaborated with the occupying power from apprehension or indifference. They too now lived in shame. Klaus could feel for them, as he always felt for the weak and the defeated, but he couldn't endure their company. The thought that they had attended parties at the German embassy and fawned on the men in uniform they met there disgusted him.

But so too did the new lords of the intellect, with their Pope, Sartre, who preached a diluted version of the philosophy of the Nazi-sympathiser Heidegger, and who fawned on Stalin: intellectuals for whom the barbarity and persecutions of the Soviet Union were of no account, because they still believed, or affected to believe, that a new earthly Paradise was being created there.

Klaus had gone to Moscow for a Congress in 1934 and found much to disturb him: the militarism and the subservience expressed by the man who said, "I do whatever the Party decides I should do": it was no different from Fascism, he had decided. And then there was the essential triviality of orthodox Marxism, its denial of so much that he valued in life; its denial of the metaphysical and its distortion of literature, reduced to being a propaganda instrument for the Faith. Besides, how could he associate himself with a regime which had once again made homosexual acts a criminal offence?

It was, he believed, Communism's reduction of life to a brutal materialism which had driven his friend and lover, the poet René Crevel, to kill himself, the night before the opening of the anti-Fascist Congress of Intellectuals in Paris which he had helped to organise.

Sitting now in the Café de la Gare Klaus leafed through his notebook till he came on the words sent him by the Communist writer Johannes Becher, who had been with René that evening in a café on the Boul' Mich': "I don't understand it. He seemed entirely normal, not in any way depressed. Only sometimes he had such a strange way of looking beyond us, into space, as if searching for something. But he couldn't find it, whatever it was..."

Whatever it was... How often Klaus had envied René, even while aggrieved because he had deserted him...

So many had taken that way out. Klaus had ventured to the gate more than once, been pulled back before he passed through it. Next time, perhaps...

Some had done it slowly, choosing to invite Death to call on them, without themselves consciously or deliberately taking the irrevocable step. There was Joseph Roth, with whom Klaus had so often sat drinking late into the night in the Café Tournon, while Roth passed from drunken ramblings to a sudden and terrifying lucidity in which this man with the capacity to enrich life for everyone but himself spoke of his immense fatigue and longing for the moment when "we step into the dark." And Klaus had then seen, in a phrase from one of Roth's own stories, "a sunny glimmer in his kind eyes", as he envisaged the moment of release, which had come by means of brandy, whisky, pernod and red wine as the beating of the war-drums sounded loud all over Europe.

The Magician had once stood at his bedroom window in the house in Poschingerstrasse and called out to Klaus about to board a taxi that would take him to the station and then ... where? He couldn't remember, but the Magician's words still sounded in his mind: "Come home, son, whenever you are miserable and forlorn." But there was no home to return to, and the Magician was living on the other side of the Atlantic, with the two people who had given Klaus unconditional love: Erika and Mielein.

In Paris there was his second father, Gide. (Or perhaps his third, for wasn't his uncle Heinrich, who had always encouraged him, the second?) If he took the train and presented himself in the apartment in the rue Vanneau, wouldn't Gide, so clear-sighted, sceptical and yet moral, so immediately responsive to all around him, offer the reinvigoration he needed?

He remembered a lunch with him on the terrace of a restaurant near the Luxembourg Gardens. Gide had talked mostly of German literature, of the sanity of

Goethe who nevertheless understood evil. “Curious that,” he said, “Prodigious really.”

Then a boy, a street urchin with an ugly sallow face and dark dancing eyes, had come by, trying to sell flowers – lilac, Klaus recalled, a bit withered, well past its best. Gide had refused the flowers but given the child money just the same, and Klaus realised that in some way the boy was hurt, even affronted, by the exchange. So, of course, did Gide: “Did you see how he looked at me?” he said. “He was glad of the money but nevertheless felt insulted. Did you ever pay a prostitute but spurn her services? She'll give you just that look. Interesting, yes? The truth is that boy would far rather have picked my pocket than accepted charity. Curious that, prodigious really…”

But he couldn't run to Gide as if he himself was a little boy who has fallen over and scarted his knees and trots to Daddy for comfort.

Yet the thought of Paris was comfort itself. It might be raining there too, it probably was, for it rains often in Paris, a city that is as much at one with melancholy weather as with summer sunshine. It was the city where he had been happiest, and he thought of the friendly shabbiness of Montmartre with nostalgia and of afternoons in those same Luxembourg Gardens: that one, for instance, when he sat on a bench gazing on the beautiful statue of the “Marchand des Masques” and was joined by a young sailor who nodded appreciatively and then said, “All the same, flesh and blood is better, isn't it,” and accompanied Klaus back to his room in the Hôtel d'Alsace, two doors along from the one where Oscar Wilde had died.

He remembered how in New York, June 14 1940, he had written in his Journal: “The Nazis in Paris, it's unimaginable. Boulevard St-Germain… Place de la

Concorde. The stamp of murderers' feet. The stuff of nightmare..."

And a couple of weeks later, 26 June.. "France is dead...One still can't believe it. It's like the death of someone very close to you. What is most frightful is not the defeat, but the treachery, the betrayal..."

As in those dark days of 1940 he worried about his friends, he recalled with horror and disgust being told a few days previously that Gide's name was on a list prepared by the State Department of French men and women who would be refused entry to the USA, as being "too radical", even though it was years since Gide, after his visit to the USSR, had recanted his expression of approval of Communism, to the fury and indignation of the Party faithful. So, from then on, he was attacked from both Left and Right, which put him, Klaus thought, in the place of honour. But of course he had come through, scepticism unimpaired. He was the most honest man Klaus had known.

What would he say now? What advice would he give? (Klaus ordered a pastis and wondered as he poured water in and watched the liquid turn cloudy...)

"So you really think that you've come to the end, dear boy? Aren't you curious about tomorrow? To see what it will bring? Is your appreciation of life's comedy quite exhausted? Oh yes, you say it is, but are you sure? Give life another chance. We shall all be a long time in the grave..."

He opened his notebook again: "'Who speaks of victory?' wrote Rilke. 'To survive is enough.'"

The train for Nice which he should have taken to catch the Paris express pulled out of the station.

VI

The Twenties when every day was an adventure expired, ushering in the brown years. When had they started thinking emigration might be necessary? There was no precise moment. The idea crept up on them like river mist, and as chilling. They were after all Germans, thoroughly German, deep-rooted, despite the Magician's Brazilian-born mother and Mielein's Jewish ancestry. But her family, like countless others, were Germans first, Jews second. It was a couple of generations since they had frequented the synagogue. Nevertheless it was Mielein who first aired the question, aired it gently, almost as if she had been proposing that they go for a picnic by the lake.

They were sitting in the garden drinking tea from the Meissen cups that were part of a set she had inherited from an aunt. It was a soft afternoon, the sun still warm but a hint of autumn chill in the air. She drew a wrap around her and said, in what was little more than a sigh, so soft was her voice, "If only this would last, Klauschen…If only."

Then she was silent and seemed to be listening, her sweet face troubled but alert, as if the horns of the Wild Hunt were sounding in the woods.

"Don't tell your father, my dear," she said, "let it be our secret. He still has confidence in the German people."

Was that before or after he delivered his "Address to the Germans" at the Beethoven-Saal in Berlin – October, 1930, Klaus thought. In that discourse he appealed to the bourgeoisie to make its peace with labour and socialism, with indeed the Social Democratic Party, in order to avoid what he called the Nazi calamity. Hardly had he said this, than a journalist wearing dark glasses leaped to his feet, obedient to Dr Goebbels' instruction to start "a little something at the Beethoven-Saal", and denounced Thomas Mann as a "liar, traitor and enemy of the German race..."

Well, the journalist (and pornographer) Arnolt Bronnen, author of a biography of the Nazi martyr, the pimp Horst Wessel, had something to prove, poor wretch.

Klaus found himself smiling at the memory, precisely because it was so disgusting and so typical of the scum that was rising to the top. For someone had put it about that Bronnen was really Bronner – and everyone knows, don't they? – that Bronner is a Jewish name Indeed, yes, Bronnen accepted that; his name had been Bronner before he changed it and Herr Bronner had indeed been a filthy Jew. However his wife, Frau Bronner, who was not at all Jewish, had cuckolded him and Arnolt was the child of that liaison and his true biological father was one hundred per cent Aryan, an upstanding representative of the Herrenvolk. It was perfect and perfectly shameless. Perhaps, Klaus thought, Goebbels himself had given him these lines.

And then there was Ricki, high-strung, adorable Ricki, with his charming terrier that wore a tinkling bell round its neck.

"It's Belshazzar's Feast," Ricki cried. "The writing is on the wall. *Mene, mene, tekel, upharsin.* Thou art weighed in the balance and found wanting. That's Jehovah's message to Germany. Everything is lost, we're done for, doomed, the whole lot of us... The Nazis will come and swallow up my little dog and Erika's sportscar and your books, Klaus – they'll burn them, don't doubt it, and my paintings which they will condemn as immoral. Oh yes, we've had it. No doubt about that. We might as well cut our throats or gas ourselves."

And then he would launch into an imitation of Hitler which was so lifelike they all burst out in horrified but irresistible laughter.

"Yes," he would say, suddenly calm, "it's not worth killing oneself on account of that little twerp."

Nevertheless that is what he did, suddenly, after a day when he had appeared unusually cheerful. He still came to Klaus often in dreams.

As for the actual moment, the turning-point in his life, January 30, 1933, Klaus had taken a train from Berlin to Leipzig where he had an appointment with the director of the City Theatre to discuss the production of one of his plays. The director, as arranged, met him at the station, and took him straight to the bar where, without asking, he ordered two large brandies.

"You're going to need this," he said.

"What's wrong? Have you decided not to do the play?"

(Oh, the egocentricity of authors!)

"It's not that. I can't believe you haven't heard the news. The old gentleman has appointed him."

"What?"

"Hitler," he said. "Hindenburg has made him Chancellor..."

Hindenburg, the senile Junker who boasted he had never read a book since his schooldays before the war of 1870, believed the assurances given him by the Conservative Nationalist Right – von Papen and the other idiots – that they could control Hitler. "He's our obedient tool," they whispered.

Some tool!

At the Nuremberg trials, Erika, there as a journalist, had observed all, and written to Klaus to say: "It's extraordinary. Von Papen still doesn't feel the burden of guilt he carries."

He got away with it too, one of the three in the dock there to be acquitted.

There was no more talk of the play, and Klaus took the next train to Munich where, for the moment, sanity still reigned. There was no Gestapo yet in Bavaria. Life still seemed close to normal. People who would have been arrested if they had remained in Berlin – Klaus himself among them – were free to amuse themselves. They flocked to Erika's cabaret show, The Peppermill, and laughed at its sharp and bitter mockery of the Nazis. Some said that if Hitler appointed a Gauleiter for Bavaria he would be arrested when he crossed the frontier. Clerical Conservative politicians and aristocrats talked of restoring the Wittelsbach monarchy and proclaiming that Bavaria had resumed its independence. They were in discussions with Prince Rupprecht, the heir to the throne. It came to nothing. He had fought bravely, they said, in the war, but now he preferred to remain on his estates, shooting game.

What a farce!

The Reichstag burned in Berlin, but in Munich they danced at the Regina Palast Hotel and the Hotel Vier Jahreszeiten. There were rumours of arrests in Berlin, of Social Democrats and Communists being hauled off to torture chambers, but tea was still drunk and strawberry tarts and apfelstrudel eaten at the Carlton. Erika arranged to transfer her cabaret to a bigger theatre, and she and Klaus slipped over the border to Switzerland for a few days' holiday.

Even when you hear the first cracks in the ice, Klaus thought, you still persuade yourself it will bear your weight. Yet every time they turned on the radio, the news was worse, more frightening and scarcely believable.

Nevertheless they went back to Munich. Erika had rehearsals to arrange, Klaus was eager to resume discussions about his new play.

The family chauffeur Hans met them at the station, as usual. But he wasn't himself.

"Don't go out," he said, "don't let anyone know you're here. Don't even telephone. The Nazis are out to get you. Especially you, Fraulein Erika."

He was sweating as he spoke.

(It was not long before Klaus understood the reason for his agitation. Hans, a nice friendly fellow, always respectful, devoted apparently to Mielein, had been a Nazi spy for years, a stoolie appointed by the Brown House to report everything that went on in the Mann family. Now he was divided between his natural decent feelings and his duty to the Party – his fear of the Party too, Klaus supposed.)

Despite the warning, Klaus went by Arcistrasse to call on his grandparents, urging them to make ready to leave Germany.

"We've lived through worse times," they said, "and we're too old, Klauschen, to uproot ourselves. Nobody will trouble themselves with relics like us. Besides what would become of our good servants if we did so?"

Fortunately the parents were already abroad in Arosa in Switzerland, the Magician having been on a lecture tour. It was necessary to call them, but, thinking it likely that the telephone was tapped, their conversation was guarded. You shouldn't come home just now. The weather's frightful in Munich. It can't be worse than it is here in Arosa, the Magician said. There's spring-cleaning going on. The house is uninhabitable for the moment. And so on. Klaus was never sure that they had grasped the full import. But Erika left to join them in Switzerland that evening.

Klaus lingered for a couple of days, making arrangements but unable to settle. He corrected a set of proofs, listened to the gramophone (*Salome*, *Kindertotenlieder*), even ventured into the city, saw a great crowd gathered in front of a villa; they were admiring Hitler's Mercedes.

Hans drove him to the station.

"Well," he said, "look after yourself. I suppose this is the last time I'll drive a member of the family. Tomorrow your car will be confiscated. It's just the thing for the Party. Don't think badly of me, Herr Klaus. Try to understand my position. A fellow must live, after all. No ill feelings, I hope."

"No ill feelings, Hans..."

He took the night train for Paris. He travelled light, only a couple of suitcases, books and magazines. He'd soon be back. The Nazi farce couldn't last. Even if the Germans didn't soon throw them out, the democracies of France and Britain would see to it: break off trade and diplomatic relations. That would be enough, surely, to bring the German people to their senses.

He shared the sleeping compartment with a young American, a nice boy on his way home who seemed unaware of anything untoward happening in Germany.

In Paris he checked into the Hôtel Jacob, discovered he had left his reading-glasses in the train and wrote to the station authorities in Munich asking them to forward them (which they did, a couple of weeks later). It didn't occur to him that it would be years before he set foot in Germany again, not even the next morning when a friend told him of another friend who had been badly beaten up in Berlin as a Jew, a foreigner and a homosexual. He went to bed and dreamed of his death and of Erika: I feel alone whenever I'm not with her.

And that was that.

He looked at his watch. Almost time to go to the Zanzi bar.

VII

Klaus had always liked bars at the hour when they were opening in the evening, when they were cool and quiet, and there was a note of expectancy in the air.

He wasn't the first to arrive in the Zanzi, but there were only half a dozen before him: a couple of Brazilian transvestites showing off improbably long legs in silk stockings; a pair of obvious rent-boys, not his type because of their blatant effeminacy, who straightway made eyes at him and then giggled when he shook his head; a stout bald man who looked as if he had come direct from his office and kept his briefcase tucked under his arm; and a middle-aged man with lank grey hair; he wore a seersucker suit and had his head buried in a book.

One of the rent-boys approached this one, sat at his table and said, "Buy me a drink, dearie."

Without looking up the man took a note from his breast-pocket, handed it over, and said in English, "Now bugger off, will you, Billie. I'm not in the mood."

"Well, if that's all you can say," Billie replied in French, picking up the note and flouncing off with a wiggle of his bottom.

Then, aware perhaps that Klaus had observed this scene, if only in truth with a detached interest and mild amusement, the man looked up, got to his feet and came over to Klaus's table.

"Mind if I join you? We've met before, long time back. In Berlin. I was a friend of Chris and he introduced us."

"Chris?"

"Isherwood, I mean. Guy Probyn. You won't remember me, I'm sure, because I was a nobody then. Actually I'm still a nobody."

He gave a sudden charming smile that took ten years off his face.

"As to that," Klaus said, "I'm surprised you recognised me."

"Oh I've seen photographs since. Besides, I was excited to meet you then. Thomas Mann's son, that made a big impression. Later I had other reasons to think about you."

"Have a drink anyway," Klaus said, and signalled to the barboy.

"Brandy," Guy Probyn said, "but they're on me."

He took a packet of Chesterfield from his pocket, shook out a cigarette and flicked a gold lighter.

"Do you still see Chris?" he said.

"In LA last year. He's all right. He's still into this Vedanta nonsense – at least I suppose it's nonsense – but he's all right. The same Chris really."

The boy brought them two generous cognacs and a soda siphon. Guy squirted a splash into his glass, and said,

"Here's to old times and the boys we knew in Berlin. Strange coincidence meeting you."

He laid his book on the table open at the title page: Klaus Mann, *Mephisto*.

Klaus didn't know what to say. Then he smiled, and lifted his glass, knocking it against Guy's.

"Cheers, as you say in England. You are English, aren't you? That's what I remember, even if your suit is American."

"Sure, I'm English, but I'm a New Yorker now. You might say I'm mid-Atlantic.

"Do you know," Klaus said," when I was young I used to dream of being in a train and finding myself opposite someone who was reading one of my books and smiling over it. It never happened, and now here you are, the dream come true. If you were smiling, that is."

"Oh sure, it's a good novel, may even be more than that. I don't know yet, I'm only halfway through."

"Are you a writer yourself? Probably I should know, but... I hope asking isn't an insult, I rather think I should know the answer."

"I'm in the theatre. I used to be an actor, but now I'm in management."

He drew on his cigarette.

"You're a bit hard on Gustaf, aren't you?"

"You think so? Did you know him?"

"Pretty well. I don't say it isn't a brilliant portrait and I won't deny it's ninety per cent true. But there's the other ten per cent. The bit you leave out. Of course, I don't know how it ends yet.."

"It hasn't ended," Klaus said. "He's still there."

"I'm talking about the novel. That's all. And the missing ten per cent."

"What do you mean?"

"I stayed on in Berlin till the end of '35. It was interesting. Hellish in many ways, but for a foreigner, an outsider, compelling viewing. We can't all be heroes. I'm positively unheroic myself. But for so many it was a question of surviving, of adapting, and Gustaf was one of those."

"He made a good job of surviving," Klaus said. "Goering's pet, Director of the State Theatre, not bad going."

"Oh sure."

Guy downed his brandy and called to the barboy for the same again.

"Oh sure, he made a good job of it. But what else was he to do? Like I said, we're not all built to be heroes. And he's an actor. He was playing the role the Reichsmarschall offered him."

"Playing it uncommonly well. Shamefully well."

"Absolutely, and he's still at it, has resurrected his career as you doubtless know, is still the idol of the

Berlin public. You have to give it to him. Whichever part is assigned to him he carries it off like the star he is."

"You sound as if you were in love with him."

"No, never that. Not my type. I prefer soft boys."

He nodded towards the two in the corner, who were now playing the table-football machine.

"You're right of course," he said. "He sold his soul. All I'm saying is that it's wrong to think he didn't suffer."

"I've never denied the suffering," Klaus said, "as you'll find if you read to the end. Nevertheless..."

He would have left it there, but Guy persisted.

"And the Princess Tebab stuff. Was that fair?"

"Fair?" Klaus said. "I wrote that novel in thirty-five, six. It's never been published in Germany, you know, though there are plans to do so now. But, as for Gustaf, would you have expected me to be fair?"

"Perhaps not, but, speaking as a man of the theatre, these passages don't ring true. Nor from what I knew of Gustaf."

"You think he wasn't a masochist, that he didn't seek humiliation as well as triumph, that both weren't necessary to him? Perhaps I knew him better than you?"

"At least you don't fall back on the pretence that Hendrik, as you call him in the novel, is only to be regarded as an imaginary character. I admire you for that, Klaus, but I still say these passages strike a false note. Sorry and all that."

"An imaginary character?" Klaus said. "You're a man of the theatre. You must know that all a writer's characters are imaginary, no matter whether they are based on real people or not. They are people as one imagines them to be."

"That's sophistry. All the more so when, like your portrait of Gustaf, they are immediately recognisable and yet false."

Klaus knew there was nothing to say. "What I have written, I have written" – that was Jehovah, wasn't it? The unforgiving God of his and Mielein's ancestors. And it was indeed in that spirit that he had pinned Gustaf to the wall of literature. Pretentious thought – this Guy Probyn would laugh if he uttered it. And what, he wondered, had he done in the war?

"Gustaf was never a Nazi," Probyn said now. "You must know that. Surely you know that. Just an actor, always an actor, and you can hardly blame him if he played all his parts well, like the great actor he is."

"I haven't denied that," Klaus said, "but he rented himself to the regime and I can't forgive. That's all there is to it."

"You hurt him, you know, wounded him badly, because he always retained an affection for you. I've heard him speak about you, with tenderness, and also with a sort of envy. Indeed even then I wondered if what he really wanted was to be Klaus Mann, not Gustaf Gründgens. It's a mixed-up world."

Klaus picked up his glass.

"Have you seen him since the war?"

"Oh yes, in Berlin last year. He spoke about you."

"Bitterly?"

"Bitter, yes, puzzled too. 'Why did he do this to me?' he said. I hadn't read this then -" he tapped the book on the table before him. "Thought I should. And, as I say, it's good, so far as I've got, but cruel. He said you sent him a copy when it was first published."

"I saw he got one, yes. It wasn't easy, on account of the censorship."

"He was awfully hurt, I think you should know that. He just couldn't understand how you could write about him as you did. And I'm puzzled too."

He picked up the book, downed his brandy, and gestured to the boy whom he had addressed as Billie.

"My sort," he said to Klaus. "Soft boy. Well, I'm glad to have met you again."

He put his arm round the boy's shoulders and whispered something in his ear. The boy giggled, and they passed through the beaded curtain and went into the night.

Klaus looked at his watch. Miki was late. Perhaps he wasn't coming. Probably he wasn't coming. What to do? He couldn't face returning to the loneliness of his hotel room. Not yet. He called for another brandy, took out his notebook.

"Julian," he wrote, "remembered an evening in a Brasserie near the Gare de l'Est – Brasserie de Strasbourg? It was his first visit to Paris since the war, and he knew himself to be more alone than he had ever been in that city which was now haunted by ghosts. There was a woman he had loved in 1938 and urged to accompany him to America. But she had refused. "Europe's too interesting," she said, and laughed. In his memory there was mockery, self mockery, in that laugh. Why hadn't she come with him? She was Jewish, a refugee from Vienna. He feared then what awaited her, though not precisely, for who, even in the weeks around Munich, had envisioned the death camps? He had made enquiries since, and learned nothing. She had made no mark in Paris, where she had lived in a tiny room on the top floor of a cheap hotel with a notice saying that cooking in rooms was forbidden. Perhaps nobody in the city now remembered her, except himself. Hers was only one of millions of lives obliterated, and when he had opened his own door to Death, it would be as if she had never lived. The waiter brought him his *choucroute* and a bottle of Sylvaner, said the perfunctory, "bon appétit, m'sieur". Julian poured himself a glass of wine, and found he had no desire for food. A family of six people at the table across the way broke out, all, simultaneously, in laughter, catching his attention. It was held longer by the boy at the end of the table nearest him. Aware of his gaze, the boy glanced across and smiled. He had brown eyes and long lashes, a soft unformed face, stocky build, like a footballer, Julian thought. Then the boy looked away, allowing Julian to take note of an exquisite profile. He was perhaps seventeen. His right leg trembled. Then his mother leaned forward and presented him with a morsel from her plate, held out on a fork. A spoilt child, the darling of the family, Julian said to himself. Later, when the party rose to go, they all embraced the boy..."

Klaus laid his pen aside. It was no good, dead as mutton. Did he believe in Julian's Jewish girl? As for the boy and his family, that was real enough, a memory drawn from his own last visit to Paris and a meal in the same Alsatian brasserie. And, as they left, the boy had turned to Klaus again and smiled, as if saying, "Yes, I know I've made an impression on you, and perhaps if things were different, who knows? But now we're going home *en famille* and we'll never see each other again." It was ridiculous and the memory was one he couldn't plausibly give to Julian, not with that suggestion of desire... And of course he himself had only imagined the boy's thoughts, which might have been quite different, as, for instance, "I know what you want, you sad old pervert..."

VIII

He wouldn't drug tonight. He could do without. It was ten days since he had left the clinic where he had endured what he called 'a clear-out' and he had only flirted with H since then. No need tonight. Three fingers of whisky and a couple of Luminal would see him through. Good, better... but best? Best was far away.

Best was in the past, when they were young and the drugs were no more than naughtiness, to give them a lift. They had all played with them, Gustaf too, despite his inherent timidity, fear that he might surrender something of himself. They called heroin "H" or "tuna", the fish that swims in the body. Erika had turned away from it. She was always the strong one. One of her letters from a long time back ran through his memory. "Don't take anymore – if you promise, I'll give it up too. It's unhealthy! It's expensive – and you can't afford it! It's dangerous, a killer – don't you realise that, my love? I embrace you from across mountains. We are too far apart from each other."

That letter gave him courage, or at least resolution. He would take a cure. He went to see Dr Katzenstein in Zurich, who frowned as he prodded him, and sighed, as if to say "Why are you young people so bent on self-destruction. Look outside, at the blue sky and the mountains. Isn't life beautiful? Isn't it good?" Perhaps he actually spoke these words, didn't merely look them. Klaus couldn't remember if he himself had put them in the mouth of the good doctor who, however, recommended that he go to a sanatorium in Hungary, in a town called – delicious irony – Siesta.

Klaus assented. The truth was that for the first time in his life he was frightened, really afraid. This was absurd. After all, didn't he often dream of death, and wasn't he, by agreeing to go to the sanatorium, running away from what he deep down most desired? Yet there was sufficient reason. It was 1937, and to will death now would be a sort of desertion. Two things gave meaning to his life: writing and the struggle against the Brown Plague, a struggle which, admittedly, he carried on only in words. So, yes, he would check in (as the Americans said) to the sanatorium and force himself to go on living.

But first he had gone to Prague because the Czech President Benes had had the courage to defy the Nazis and offer passports to the entire Mann family, stateless since their German ones had been withdrawn. (Well, not to Erika, who was in no need of one, on account of her *mariage blanc* to Wystan Auden which made her British. Klaus had first proposed on her behalf to Chris, but he had said no because he saw marriage as a prop of what he called 'the heterosexual dictatorship' and in any case his boy-friend Heinz would be hurt and wouldn't understand. So he "passed the buck" to Wystan who, like the English gentleman he was, consented, even though, unlike Chris, he had never met Erika. Years later, in America, someone asked the Magician who Chris was. "Family pimp," he replied).

It was in recognition of the Magician's status that the Czech offer was made. Well, this was one time when Klaus wasn't in the least reluctant to cling to his father's coat-tails! He went to Prague and had an interview with the President himself, whom he found to be lively, intelligent and professorial. Their conversation had been almost entirely political, and therefore bleak. They both knew that while times were bad, worse lay ahead.

He had to wait in Budapest, where he stayed in a palace owned by a friend, the Baron Lazi von Hatvany, twice exiled from his own country for his liberal views, first by Reds, then by the quasi-Fascist dictatorship of Admiral Horthy. Now Lazi, permitted to return, didn't know how long his reprieve would last. Klaus had interviews with doctors, one of whom, Klopstock, had been a close friend of Kafka and had indeed held him in his arms as he died. Klopstock liked to speak about literature, but then, after giving Klaus a physical examination, asked him: "So why do you drug?"

"Because I wanted to die. I am attracted to death."

"You said 'wanted' – past tense. So you no longer want to die and are ready to undergo the cure – disintoxication. It's painful, you know."

"What isn't?" Klaus might have said, but he only nodded his head.

"You have a reason to live now?"

"I don't know. I hope so."

But in truth there was another reason, beside the political struggle to which he was committed, though he did not dare express it. Did not dare because he couldn't yet believe in it.

At a restaurant, the Hungaria, with Lazi Hatvany and his wife, Jolan, and son Klari, he was introduced to a young American. No, that wasn't right. It was a pick-up, though later they argued as to which of them had made the approach. Not that it mattered. The boy was blond, green-eyed, smooth sunburnt face. In his journal that night Klaus wrote, cagily, of "the little Curtis, pretty kid, a bit affected, pleased with himself." And why not? He had a lot to be pleased with, and even the first exchange of glances showed him willing. He set out to impress. "I've just come from the Soviet Union where I was studying under Eisenstein." Message: I'm not one of your café boys, I'm an artist too.

The next day, or the one after, they made an excursion together to a ruined castle which had belonged to the Kings of Hungary before the Ottoman invasion. Klaus had no thought for its history, only for Curtis whom, as tribute to his Russian connection, he called Tomski. Love, he thought, true love, for the first time in years: happiness and mystery. They went to a hotel: his nervousness, his sadness, his intelligence, his tenderness, his sensuality, his laughter, his sighs, his lips, his eyes, his body, his strong well-shaped legs, his smooth arms, his voice with the intoxicating drawl of the American South.

Klaus stretched out on his bed and recalled those first hours: perfection, sought so long, fleetingly caught.

"But you must," Tomski said, "go through with this cure. I've heard what drugs can do. You must go through with it for our future."

Our future? When had anyone last spoken of that to him, in those soft and certain tones?

Would he have done it if Tomski hadn't urged him? He would never know. It was the sort of question that was by its nature unanswerable. When you came to the crossroads and followed one arm of the signpost, the alternative route, the one not taken, was wiped out. He had known that for years. Yet he also knew that if Tomski had laughed and said, "Don't bother. Come away with me tomorrow," he would have abandoned the sanatorium and left with the boy.

They put him in a room with barred windows. He made it his by laying out the photographs of family, friends, lovers he carried with him on his wanderings. Visitors forbidden. Tomski was allowed ten minutes to say goodbye. They kissed and it was like being left on an empty platform watching the train pull away. No visitors, the injunction was repeated. "We can never be certain," the nurse said, "that out of mistaken kindness they won't smuggle in drugs." All the same that first night they gave him a little heroin, the smallest shot, along with pills, to allow him to sleep.

He did so, for a few hours, and woke tired, weak, nervous and afraid. But it could be endured...

Months later in his novel *Der Vulkan*, he relived the ordeal through his hero, Martin: "All around him was twitching feet and hands jerked themselves into spasms. He threw his tormented head about. He would never have thought he could be simultaneously so exhausted and so tremblingly alive. He was too weak to get out of bed, but his wet, quivering body couldn't bear to be in the same position for thirty seconds. He had been ill often, as a child especially, but nothing like this. In comparison fever and bodily pain were positive feelings. This was a huge embarrassment. 'It's how a fish must feel, when it's been thrown on land,' Martin thought. 'With the hook still in its mouth. I'm wriggling like a fish on dry land. My God, my God, what have I done that I must flap about like a wretched little fish...'"

Der Vulkan... His best novel? Perhaps. His most ambitious? Certainly. It sold only three hundred copies.

He gave himself another whisky. Why not? An old friend that kept the temptation of H at arm's length.

Never mind. That novel brought him something worth more than sales: the Magician's approval. He had never believed that his father did more than glance through his books – and that only because Mielein insisted he should read them. But this time the Magician wrote: "Well then: fully and thoroughly read it and it touched me and made me laugh. I enjoyed it and was really satisfied and more than once I was really moved. For a long time now people didn't take you seriously – they saw you as the 'son-of' (T. Mann's little boy), a spoiled brat. I couldn't change that. But now it's not to be denied that you are capable of more, more than most – therefore my satisfaction on reading and my other emotions rightfully stem from that too. In a word, I congratulate you sincerely and with fatherly pride..."

And, further on, reflecting on the passage in which Klaus recounted his hero's cure in the sanatorium, the Magician wrote that he found it "so extraordinary a piece of narrative that I stopped thinking about Germany and morality, politics and struggle, and just read on because I had never read anything like it before."

For a long time he carried that letter wherever he went, as you might wear a badge of honour. He had never had such praise from the Magician before, for even *Mephisto* had been met with a bland approval betraying a lack of real interest. In truth he hadn't realised how much he needed his father's praise, which in his reply he described as "a beautiful, comforting, and fortifying gift..."

But the cure itself – terrible, as he had written. Nights of agitation, brief sleep, disturbed by horrible and frightening dreams. When he woke sobbing, a nurse came and sat by him and spoke of her broken marriage. There's misery everywhere, he thought. Later he spent two whole days asleep (with the help of pills), but when he woke, found himself not rested, but exhausted, hardly able to walk. Cries of anguish came from the neighbouring rooms. Did it help that others were suffering as he was?

At last letters arrived, from Erika, promising to be with him in person as she was in spirit, from Mielein, to whom he had confessed all in a letter written the day before he began the cure. Hers was full of sympathy, understanding and love. It made him weep. But tears came very easily in the room with barred windows. There were more when Tomski was at last permitted to visit and brought him roses and kisses. Left alone, night drawing on, he had moments of rebellion. "Je m'en fous," he wrote in his journal. "My head is strangely empty of everything."

He was ready to leave, but the doctors said no. A few days yet. You must be stronger, the poison completely eliminated. Tomski sat by the bed and held his hand or smoothed his brow. Gave him lemonade to drink. The boy himself veered between joy and despair. Like Rene, he thought, like René and Rikki.

When at last he was released after a month in the sanatorium, Klopstock and another doctor came to the station to see him off. "Don't come back, Klaus," they said. "You've given yourself another chance. Don't come back." In the train Tomski smiled and said, "Now we are truly together." They spent that night in the Hotel Imperial in Vienna, in each other's arms. Klaus wept, but they were tears of happiness.

He sat by the window, with his glass of whisky and the bottle of Johnnie Walker on the table by his side. No. he wouldn't drug tonight. It was strangely peaceful watching the rain still falling. There had been good times with Tomski often, and over a number of years, but never as good as those first weeks together, when he asked himself time and again, can I love him enough? Of course he couldn't. That was, as the English said, "the fact of the matter". He couldn't love anyone enough. His own need was too great.

Guy Probyn had set out to rile him, no question of that. Why? Not just to defend Gustaf, but also because there was something in Klaus himself which invited attack. Or was Probyn, with his attraction to soft boys whom he could dominate, merely malicious, full of the resentment of the man who would have been an artist and was now a manager? Klaus took hold of the bottle and smiled. Was it possible that Probyn was jealous of him? Ridiculous thought. He poured another whisky, but didn't immediately drink it. Sufficient comfort to know it was there waiting, ready when his need became urgent.

There was a knock at the door. He didn't answer at once. He hesitated because for a moment he had been close to happiness in his solitude and didn't want it to be interrupted. But the knock was repeated and this time he called, "Come in". It was Miki.

"I got held up on the boat," he said. "The boss had insisted we put to sea."

He came up behind Klaus, laid his hands on his shoulders and leant over him. He smelled of the rain and there was again aniseed on his breath.

"You OK, Klaus? They told me you'd been at the Zanzi. So I came on the chance. Are you pleased?"

Klaus emptied his glass, got up, turned round, ran his hands up the boy's body under his shirt.

"I'm pleased," he said, and kissed him on the mouth.

Rainwater dripped down his neck from Miki's hair.

"It's good to see you," Klaus said. "I was sad when I gave you up."

IX

The sun was shining for the first time that month and Klaus's spirits rose with it. He felt better than he had for days. Miki's arrival had helped change his mood. Klaus was touched that the boy had sought him out. Of course he wanted money – it was rent after all – but Klaus persuaded himself there was affection there too. When the boy kissed him goodbye in the morning and said again, "you're all right, Klaus," he was able, almost, to persuade himself that the words were true.

He had an engagement: lunch with Mr Maugham at the Villa Mauresque on Cap Ferrat. Yesterday he had thought he would let it slip, though he had found the English novelist sympathetic when they had met in New York during the war. That was soon after he had seen the film made from Maugham's novel *Of Human Bondage*, starring Leslie Howard and Bette Davis. It hadn't entirely convinced him; it wasn't altogether plausible that the young man should have succumbed so completely to that monstrous woman. All the same he had noted in his Journal that he found it interesting that, on the evidence of the movie – for Klaus hadn't then read the novel – Maugham should have made this pathological submission to an inferior woman a symbol of the homosexual condition. For he had no doubts about Mr Maugham's own sexuality; he was an unbridled Magician, and there was something demonic in his understanding of infatuation with an unsuitable object.

He took a train to Nice and then, unable to afford a taxi, a bus which deposited him at the bottom of the hill leading up to the villa. A butler wearing white gloves admitted him, and Klaus was conscious of the shabbiness of his suit and the fact that it hadn't occurred to him to wear a tie. Then to his dismay he found there were other guests, an English couple, whose names he didn't catch but they were Lord and Lady something, and a dark boy with loose lips who immediately gave him the eye. Not his type however, with willowy gestures which repelled. Very dry Martinis were served, and promptly at one o'clock the butler struck a gong to summon them to lunch. Klaus found himself beside Mr Maugham's secretary-manager – former lover? procurer? – Alan Searle who talked about criminals he had known in an accent Klaus found hard to place. The food was bland – fish in a velvety sauce, followed by indifferent roast chicken. But the wine was good, though the supply was stinted. Maugham himself smoked, not only between courses, and picked at his food. Breaking a moment of silence, the English lady asked him what had been the happiest moment of his life.

"When I finally got rid of my wife," he said, his stammer delaying the "finally" and the "got", the last words "rid of my wife" emerging in a rush.

Klaus couldn't think why he had been asked. He felt an imperative need for heroin. A popular American song of the twenties ran in his head: "I'm just a bird in a gilded cage." That, surely, was Mr Maugham. He longed for the moment of departure, but, when the other guests were at last ready to leave, after coffee had been served and the two Pekingese provided with sugared biscuits, Alan Searle sidled up to him and said, "He'd like you to stay behind, he wants the opportunity to talk. Please do. It will give me an hour to myself."

The willowy boy lingered too, but was abruptly dismissed by Mr Maugham.

"Find something with which to amuse yourself, if you're capable of that. You might even read a book."

He took Klaus by the arm and led him on to the terrace and then down some steps to the pool where there were chairs and a table under an awning.

Maugham said, "One of the misfortunes of human beings is that they continue to have sexual desires long after they are no longer sexually desirable. That won't have struck you yet..."

His stammer had difficulty with "desires" and "desirable".

"Are you intending to start another magazine?"

Klaus sighed and said, "It's impossible."

"Your New York one was good. I was happy to contribute to it, though my essay was perhaps a bit dry."

"It was an honour to publish it," Klaus said, and wondered how soon he could take his leave without causing offence. He didn't like speaking about that magazine – *Decision*. He had started it with such high hopes and it had fizzled out so ignominiously.

"And the other Germany, of which you and your sister wrote? Will that be realised? Is it a country you could live in again?"

Klaus shook his head. Germany was tainted, he said; he couldn't look anyone in the eye there without seeing guilt.

"A pity," Maugham said. "I spent two years of my youth in Heidelberg, you know. I discovered myself there and so I have always kept an affection for that Germany. It was the first place where I made friends who mattered to me. You understand?"

Yes, Klaus understood, but it was not something he thought he could speak of with this elderly Englishman who seemed on the brink of confidences which could only embarrass them both.

"Life is a comedy to those who think, a tragedy to those who feel. You know the quotation? What's your opinion?"

Suddenly Klaus was close to tears. He remembered how when the magazine failed he had wished to die because he could no longer endure the mass of mediocrity and malice, and how writing down his long litany of complaint had somehow diverted him from the suicide he had that evening been planning. Now he felt that this wise old man understood him and had asked him here, not merely as a courtesy but because he had sensed, got wind of, his desperation and had something important to tell him.

"But can you divorce thought and feeling?" he said. "Make that clear distinction between them? Isn't every thought a feeling too, every feeling a thought at least when you find words for it?"

"And so," Maugham said, "tragicomedy... Of course, Faust is the great German myth, as both you and your father have realised. To sell your soul to satisfy your immediate desires. No Frenchman would do that without counting the cost, but then no Frenchman is a Romantic. Your father's novel is remarkable. He must be very sure of himself to dare to bore the reader as he does. I would never have had the courage. But I preferred your *Mephisto* because it shows how easily a man may sell his soul, even for a low price. The Germans surrendered their souls to Hitler willingly, even eagerly, but how many of them really believed in his promises? They could do so only by suspending the critical and sceptical spirit. Yet they rushed to do that. You stood out against the mass delusion, but do you truly suppose that your words achieved anything?"

There was ancient malice in his voice, common sense in the words.

"No," Klaus said, "I can't believe that they did. But I couldn't not have written them."

"Has your novel been published in Germany?"

"You mean *Mephisto*? No, but I hope it may be soon."

"It should be. Your compatriots – or should I say, your former compatriots? – need such books. I mean, books that open their eyes to the manner in which they surrendered to evil. Not, I fear, that people learn from books, or from experience. But they should be given the opportunity. You were in love once with the character you call Hendrik?"

"Yes," Klaus said. He suddenly wanted to unburden himself to this wise old man.

"I thought so. Such hatred and contempt are born only from love that has turned sour."

A cloud passed over the sun. The old man's face darkened. Klaus thought he was looking into that cupboard under the stairs where unwanted memories are hidden away, but can't be forgotten.

The willowy boy emerged from the house, descended the steps. He was wearing a dressing-gown, which he slipped off without looking at either of them, and stood at the edge of the pool in ersatz leopard-skin trunks. He raised himself on his toes, then lay flat on his belly and pulled up first one leg, then the other, behind him.

Maugham said, "For many years I was ambitious to make a mark in the world. Now I regard that as futility. I still work every morning, but it is for my own amusement now, or simply because it is an occupation to stave off boredom. But I no longer look for applause."

The boy stood up and dived into the water. When he surfaced he brushed his hair out of his eyes and looked towards Maugham. Or perhaps Klaus himself, he couldn't be sure. Getting no response, he turned away, swam across the pool using the crawl stroke, climbed out and lay flat face-down on stone. The sun came out and the boy's wet legs glistened.

"My nephew Robin left him here," Maugham said. "He supposed I would be grateful. He was mistaken."

Klaus said, "I'm afraid I must be off."

He had in reality no reason to go, but he knew he couldn't remain there a moment longer.

"You work in the morning," he said, "for me the best time is late afternoon and early evening."

Why did he always feel the need to make some excuse, offer some explanation?

"Just remember," Maugham said, "nothing matters very much and most things don't matter at all."

Klaus looked at his watch.

"If I go now, I can just catch the next bus at the bottom of the hill."

He thanked Maugham. They shook hands. As he turned out of the gate, he encountered Alan Searle. Searle was puffing, out of breath.

"You're off then. Hope your little talk went all right. Is the old man alone?"

"He's by the pool," Klaus said. "The boy's there, sunning himself."

"Ah good," Searle said. "I'm pleased to hear it. Willie doesn't like to be left alone. Except when he's working of course."

X

He had sailed to America with Tomski only a few months after his release from the clinic. He wasn't abandoning the anti-Nazi struggle, and yet part of him accused himself of doing precisely that. It was nonsense. He was a writer and he could carry on his war in words either side of the Atlantic. Moreover, Erika had secured an agent who would arrange a lecture tour for the pair of them. That was how they could immediately best serve the cause – by telling Americans the truth about what was happening in Germany and persuading them that they could not stand apart from the assault on democracy and civilisation.

So why did he feel like a deserter?

Because, even with the streets of American cities still bearing witness to the number of men whom the Depression had left without work, the US yet seemed to him a land of endless possibility, free of the gnawing anxiety you couldn't escape in Europe.

Journalists and photographers met the ship. As Thomas Mann's son he was news. A reporter from the New York Post asked him about his love life. Klaus looked him in the eye and recognised him as "one of us". He can read what there is between me and Tomski, he thought, and in reply referred first to his broken engagement to Pamela and then in vague terms to an attachment to a girl in Switzerland – in reality Annemarie who had been Erika's lover off and on for years.

"So you see," Tomski said as soon as they were alone, "even in the Land of the Free, you can't speak honestly."

Later that night Tomski was still sulky. He made a scene. They had their first quarrel. It was absurd: Tomski was no more able openly to confess to their relationship than he could… In a few days he would be going home to his parents, whom he hadn't seen for the three years he had been in Europe, and he certainly wasn't going to tell them that he had travelled to the States with his lover, a thirty-year-old German called Klaus. And yet Klaus understood the boy's resentment. They ought to have been able to say what they were. Instead, he found himself making excuses.

"If I confessed to being what I am nobody would listen to what I have to say about Hitler and the Nazis. They would dismiss me as a degenerate."

"Is that what you think we are?" Tomski said.

"You know it's not. Please don't be silly."

The quarrel went on for hours, and Klaus was the more hurt because he knew that Tomski knew his argument was ridiculous. He wondered if Tomski really wanted to find an excuse to break with him.

A couple of years later – he couldn't remember exactly when – he had a similar conversation with Chris in California.

"You don't understand," Klaus said. "I'm not ashamed of being homosexual. It's my nature and that's all there is to it. But I'm not militant, I don't need to shout it from the rooftops..."

"And you weren't ashamed to pretend?" Chris said.

"Yes, to some extent I was ashamed. I don't like telling lies. But I'd come to America not as a refugee – though I suppose I was that too – but to try to tell the American people what the Nazis are really like and to tell them that they also must one day be ready to go to war against the Brown Plague. It wasn't a popular message then, you know. Indeed it still isn't. What chance would I have had of being heard if I had announced that I was a homosexual and that the boy standing beside me was my lover? We all have to pretend."

"Not me," Chris said. "I made a resolution long ago that I am never going to deny what I am. I'm not going to submit to the heterosexual dictatorship."

Even then Klaus wondered if Chris revealed his homosexuality to the studio bosses in Hollywood. But he didn't mention his doubts. The truth was he admired Chris's defiant attitude and often wished he could match it. But then he thought: we're different, our position, if not condition, is different. Chris has renounced the political struggle and become a pacifist. How, he asked me, could he fire a gun at a German soldier when that soldier might be Heinz, who had been compelled to return to Germany because attempts to get him another passport had failed, who had been sentenced to a prison term on account of his relations with Chris and was, he believed, now in the army?

So perhaps in their incompatibility they were both right. He couldn't argue against the position Chris had adopted, but he didn't think Chris justified in condemning his.

Was it then or another day they had talked about Maugham?

No matter. He recalled the conversation as the bus carried him away from the Villa Mauresque and the sun slid behind a cloud and it began to rain again.

Perhaps it was later, after Maugham had visited Chris in California in connection with his novel *The Razor's Edge*, which was being made into a film. People said the main character, Larry Something, who travels East in search of spiritual wisdom was based on Chris. Sometimes he denied it indignantly, "He's such a twerp, that Larry, a ridiculously romanticised figure and anyway he's hetero, even if it's obvious the old man was in love with him. Actually that makes it worse because he lacked the honesty and courage to admit it." Sometimes he giggled and said, "Well, if the old boy did model him on me, he botched the job."

All the same Chris was fond of Maugham, whom he referred to often as "darling Willie". He had reason to be grateful to him, Klaus remembered, for Maugham had once been heard to say, "That young man holds the future of the English novel in his hands," which delighted Chris naturally, even if it again reduced him to giggles. "Such a responsibility. I'm afraid I'll drop it," he said.

Anyway Chris reported that on one of these occasions Maugham had come close to tears as he said, "The tragedy of my life is that I have pretended I was three-quarters normal and only a quarter queer whereas really it was the other way round from the start..."

"Actually, "Chris said, "I don't believe he's even a quarter hetero. The old darling's lived a lie all his life. No wonder he's unhappy."

Perhaps it was after the death of his lover and companion Gerald – Alan Searle's predecessor – that Maugham had come out with this anguished confession. But how else could he have lived, granting his ambition? He had been twenty or so, hadn't he, when Wilde was sent to prison, and he knew very well that he walked a dangerous path and that people wouldn't have staged his plays or bought his books if they had known him to be as he was. In any case Chris had danced on the same tightrope. You had to read between the lines in his Berlin books and that earlier novel, *The Memorial*, which Klaus loved, to know that he was queer. In the Berlin stories he had even lent his boyfriend Otto, Heinz's predecessor, to another character, a weedy and neurotic Englishman. Klaus had actually been more open in some of his own novels, though not *Mephisto*.

Then Chris, with that outspoken frankness which, even after he had known him for years, still took Klaus by surprise, because it seemed to him so un-English, said, "Your father's the same, isn't he?"

Difficult to explain that this was a misconception, difficult because of the kernel of truth which both Klaus and Erika had long recognised. But it was wrong all the same, and not only because the Magician truly loved Mielein, as well as needing her, and theirs was a happy marriage, unlike what he had learned of Maugham's.

The Magician had sublimated the homoeroticism which therefore played a bigger part in his work and perhaps his imagination than in his daily or conscious life. He kept his blond boys in his heart, perhaps, but at a distance. Not even kisses. The furthest he had gone with the other Klaus (Heuser) was admitted in a letter addressed to both Erika and Klaus to whom he gave his childhood name Eissi: "I call him 'Du'," he said of Hauser, "and at parting pressed him to my heart with his express consent." Then mischievously he added, "Eissi is requested to step back and not disturb my circles. I'm already old and famous, and why should the two of you alone be permitted to sin?" But there was of course no sin, except in his imagination, and as for the warning, it was superfluous. Young Hauser hadn't been Klaus's type. This teasing, self-teasing, restraint, was very different from Mr Maugham, who had come close to giving himself away only in one novel, *The Narrow Corner* which was, unsurprisingly, Klaus's favourite among those of his books which he had read. In fact the Magician had made his position clear in a table of qualities or attributes he had once drawn up. Klaus had it by heart:

Homoeroticism	Marriage
Art	Life
Death	Life
Artistry	Bourgeoisie
Aesthetics	Ethics, morality

Barren, childless	Fertile, procreative
Vagabond, licentious	Bourgeois life, fidelity
Individualistic	Social
Irresponsibility	Life obedient
Pessimism	Life willing, conformist
Orgiastic liberty	Commitment, duty

Certain words in the first column flew like arrows to Klaus's heart: death, barren, vagabond, pessimism... But in truth that column described him precisely. He'd known that for a long time. As for the qualities listed in the other column, he might lay claim only to "commitment, duty". Surely the tenacity of his opposition to the Brown Plague and the little rat Hitler proved that entitlement?

The bus deposited him in the square in front of the railway station. Half-an-hour to wait before the next train back to Cannes. He made for the bar, quickly from old habit surveyed it, found no one to interest him, and ordered a whisky-and-soda.

The remarkable thing was that, whereas he had only despised and loathed the little rat, the Magician, while describing him as "a catastrophe, no doubt about that", had nevertheless made the effort to understand him, declared that was "no reason to find him uninteresting as character and destiny" – as a phenomenon also, of course. Klaus had been shocked when he first read that essay and found his father calling the little rat "Brother Hitler". How could he? Well, first because he had been able to say "Where I am, there is Germany," and, being German, he could not deny Hitler's Germanity. It was something we all had in common, no matter how horrifying the realisation might be. But there was more to it than that. The man was a disaster, certainly, with his unfathomable resentment and his festering vindictiveness, but he was also a failed artist, and therefore in a sense indeed his Brother. The young Hitler had been the half-baked Bohemian in his garret or Viennese doss-house, with his basically-I'm-too good-for-ordinary-work, and his sense of being reserved for something special, indefinable, which, if he had expressed it then, would have had those around bursting out in derisive laughter. This rejection, common to that experienced by so many young artists who feel on the cusp of greatness but are recognised by nobody, fed his rage against the world, his ferociously anxious need to justify himself, his urge to compel the world to accept him at his own valuation, to subject itself to him, to satisfy his dream of seeing those who had spurned him now prostrate before him. Lost in fear, admiration and a wild besotted love. Moreover, the Magician had insisted, Hitler's insatiable drive for compensation for the miseries he had endured, his inability ever to be content with what he had achieved, and the need to proceed ever further and more dangerously on the path he had chosen, these too were attributes of the artist. "There is a lot of Hitler in Wagner," the Magician had once said to Klaus during the war. "The rejection of reason and bourgeois ethics, and the incapacity for irony – irony which is the saving grace of the intellect." If the Magician was right, Hitler was the artist's shadow-self, the dark side of the moon.

And of course the will to self-destruction. Only Klaus felt no need to pull down the whole world with him. No *Götterdämerung* for him, an overdose would do the trick. He went to the bar and asked for another whisky.

Light was fading when he was back in Cannes. The poignant loneliness of dusk. It was Miki's night with his girl again. No point in going to the Zanzi, and indeed good reason not to: Probyn might be there. He couldn't face that. He found another bar, a place on the terrace. There was a German couple at the next table. How strange to hear his language spoken here, spoken confidently, as if the war was so far behind them all, a mere parenthesis in history. The waiter brought him his whisky and a soda siphon. He took out his notebook and wrote:

"Albert's faith in Communism had been absolute, his conversion as abrupt and complete as St Paul's on the road to Damascus. One day he had been lost, and not only because his girlfriend had walked out on him because, she said, he believed in nothing and stank of petit-bourgeois failure; the next it was as if he stood on the bluff of a hill, gazing across the river and a landscape with classical ruins like a Poussin painting towards the golden light of a new dawn, the Promised Land. It was in a mood of exhilaration that he had accepted an invitation to the First Congress of Soviet Writers in Moscow. (The invitation had itself come as a surprise because he had published so little, but the editor of an exiles' magazine published in Amsterdam had recommended him.) What he found there was what he longed to find: a dynamic faith. It was marvellous to observe the joyful determination and zest with which the ordinary Soviet citizens participated in the collective effort to build Socialism. Literature in the USSR was not, as it was in the west, the occupation of a dilettante minority, a diversion for the bourgeoisie. On the contrary! It was recognised and promoted as an integral part of this vast creation of a New Society, a comprehensive scheme which appealed no less to the public imagination and general interest than the enactment of the Five-Year Plan and the reorganisation of Soviet agriculture into collective farms. The Conference offered a magnificent demonstration of this national concern for Literature. All its sessions were attended by workers, private soldiers and peasants who engaged with intelligence and enthusiasm in discussions about modern poetry and the role of the theatre and the cinema under Socialism. Albert felt his heart swell with joy. Tears of happiness came to his eyes."

Yes, indeed, these had been Klaus's own feelings, which he now lent to Albert, when he had attended that Congress and been, for a few days, enraptured, delighted too by the reverence with which all present, it seemed, regarded Maxim Gorki, and the affection, love really, they extended to the old doyen of Russian and Soviet literature. And Klaus had met other Soviet writers there like the delicate and thoughtful poet Boris Pasternak, who had charmed him. At first, that year – it was 1934 – the atmosphere, so different from that in Germany, being full of hope not hatred – had seemed intoxicating.

Intoxicating – that was actually the right word – for even before he left Moscow Klaus was experiencing the lucid revulsion of hangover. There had been an air of make-believe. People smiled to conceal their fear. There was, he realised, the same will to power there, and the OGPU was in reality no different from the Gestapo. It had been a relief to him when, a couple of years later, Gide had retracted his approval of the Stalinist regime.

And then in '38 Klaus and Erika had gone to Spain to report from the Loyalist side in the Civil War. Should he send Albert there? No, that wouldn't do, because it would have been impossible for an honest man, such as he was determined Albert should be, to have spent time in Spain without realising how viciously and unscrupulously the Communists, instructed by Moscow, had set out to destroy the democratic parties of the Republic. Why should this have surprised Klaus? It was natural it should horrify him, certainly, but why the surprise? Hadn't the Communists in Germany also obeyed orders to attack the Social Democrats and undermine support for them – because Stalin believed that they, rather than the Nazis, were the chief obstacles to Revolution? Stalin had underestimated Hitler and the Nazis. Klaus couldn't forgive him, even though he admitted that he had made the same mistake himself. "That afternoon in the Carlton tea room," he scribbled in the margin. "What a blind fool I was!"

One of the Germans at the nearby table was speaking more loudly now.

"Of course," he said, "I experienced difficulties. It seems absurd now, but I was actually hauled before one of these courts, required to prove that I had never been a member of the Party. It was because I had served in the SS, but the Waffen SS, the fighting troops, not Heinrich's boys, you understand. I enlisted because I was a German and a patriot, even though I never thought the ideology anything but rubbish. All that True Aryan stuff – it was nonsense, I always knew that. But I showed them my wound – this I got at Stalingrad, I said, fighting for Germany, not for the Nazis. Naturally they believed me, I come from a good family after all. And so I've remade my life, in our family business, which is a reputable one, believe me, and now I can say confidently that we are making a success of it. No surprise there: we Germans are after all the most efficient race in the world. Believe me, my friend, in the new Europe that must some day be constructed, we shall take the lead, even if we have for a time to disguise our mastery..."

Klaus turned to look at him. A perfectly ordinary man, a bit fleshy, but with a frank open face, well dressed, nothing repulsive about him, giving the impression of contentment, as if the twelve years of the Reich had been no more than a regrettable experience, something to be put behind him, like a bad dream the memory of which you shake off as soon as you've had your breakfast coffee. No doubt he thought that no one on the terrace understood German. Or perhaps he didn't care. Why should he? He had come through. The war was behind him and there was business to be done.

Not for the first time Klaus reproached himself for his own failure fully to comprehend the depth of the national psychosis. The truth was that he had been too bound up in his own life, which was certainly interesting enough, to bother to do so. He had been bored and disgusted by the savage boasts, but not sufficiently frightened. He hadn't grasped the brutality that went hand in hand with resentment and an inferiority complex. Instead he had travelled giving lectures on European culture and amusing himself – and his audiences – with flippant dismissal of the brown-shirted barbarians. Extraordinary though it was, he couldn't acquit himself of complacency. But then, he thought, what could he acquit himself of?

To be fair to himself, something he had always found difficult, he had learned at last. It was the young actor who taught him the lesson, the young actor to whom in *Mephisto* he gave the name of Hans Miklas. He had known him in Hamburg where he was a junior member of the company, an angry and resentful one, with his poverty, his undernourished physique, his hollow cheeks and his too-red lips. Klaus had been immediately attracted to him – the boy was so evidently unhappy. Even his ferocious jealousy of Gustaf had been appealing. At first, anyway. But the attraction was quickly replaced by disgust, for young Hans – which wasn't his real name but for a moment Klaus couldn't remember what that had been – was, he learned, a Nazi, had indeed joined the Party's Youth Movement as soon as he was able to, had done so originally to spite his father, an elementary schoolteacher and a Social Democrat. In the theatre canteen, after a single glass of beer, he would hold forth against Jews and plutocrats and the degenerates who were destroying Germany and corrupting German youth. Klaus soon understood that he was included among them. And yet, mingled with his disgust, there was pity. The boy was so horribly sincere and also idealistic; he really believed that, when Hitler had made, as he put it, "a clean sweep of that mob", a new purer Germany would be born. "Yes," he said, "whatever you think, the future belongs to us, and it will be a new world, one that is clean and honest and noble."

What a fool! But there was nothing to be done about it. You couldn't possibly rescue him. There were moments when Klaus would have liked to take him in his arms and cover his face with kisses and speak soothingly to him. Impossible of course – the boy would have hit him, spat in his face. Gustaf loathed him, and took pleasure in humiliating him at rehearsal. "Not like that, you dolt. Are you a clod-hopping peasant?. Like this, with an airy elegance, that's what your part demands. Of course, if you're not up to it, you can go back on the streets and caterwaul with your Nazis. You're a joke, but I'm not going to allow you to destroy my production. Now do it again, if you can…" That sort of thing. And the poor boy, now blushing, now pale and quivering as if he had just been told his mother was dead, repeated the required movements again and again, until at last Gustaf said, "I can teach you, but can you learn, that's the question. Well, we'll find out the answer at to-morrow's rehearsal…"

Yes, Klaus thought, it was the young Hans – no, Malte, that was his real name – he'd called him Hans because it seemed to fit his so ordinary resentful sense of being underprivileged – well, then, it was Malte who spouted the Nazi slogans – and really believed in them, he must allow him that – but it was Gustaf with his bullying and the relish he took in it who was, fundamentally, the real Nazi. With his solipsism too, his conviction that nothing mattered in the world but himself and the achievement of his goal, which was fame. Klaus wished he had spoken to Guy Probyn of Gustaf's treatment of young Malte who had incidentally been hopelessly in love with the young actress Ulrika, who had eyes only for Gustaf; it might have opened the Englishman's eyes to Gustaf's true nature.

Klaus had treated the boy well in the novel. He had allowed him to be disillusioned early, to see that he'd been betrayed, that his once-beloved Fuehrer had wanted power and nothing else. He'd had him speak out, utter his disappointment and distress, and he'd had the Nazi thugs bump him off because he was proving an embarrassment.

In reality he had no idea what had become of Malte, had never seen him after those Hamburg days and didn't know if he had indeed lost his faith. Quite probably he hadn't. But it was artistically right that the character Hans should have done so, and it was also an act of generosity on Klaus's part to have written that end for him. It was an expression of the strange tenderness he had felt for this boy whose repulsive ideas seemed at odds with what Klaus sensed was his true nature. Because this was the truly horrible thing, which he had taken so long to understand: that an unhappy idealistic boy like Malte could respond not only sincerely to the siren call of Hitler, but in a sense generously, since he truly believed or had persuaded himself that a Nazi revolution would open the window on a better world. And it wasn't as if he had been the fool Gustaf called him. On the contrary, there had been moments when he seemed really intelligent to Klaus. He wondered now what had become of him. He was probably dead. Or was he like the man at the next table, prospering and assuring the world that he had nothing to be ashamed of?

Klaus signalled to the waiter, paid his bill and set off for his hotel. The air was soft now, but thinking of the boy Malte had set his nerves on edge. Back in his room, he took out the syringe and gave himself a shot. Just a small one, to settle himself, only a small one, not enough to count as a relapse...

XI

It was raining again on a scudding wind. Klaus scribbled in his diary, “I feel bad, bad, bad. When I read over the novel I find it bad also, terribly bad, dead, rotten as last year’s fruit. I must begin again. But have I the courage?” It was all he could do to hold the pen. The writing was scarcely legible. No matter; it was for himself alone. His nerves were a-jangle. Suddenly he found himself laughing. It was too ridiculous, the thought of that bland confident German businessman at the café last night, a loser who had prospered, whereas he who had entered Germany in the triumphant American army… It didn’t bear thinking on.

He must get out, rain or not. He dressed hurriedly. Impossible to tie shoelaces. He slipped his feet into espadrilles, though they would be wet through as soon as he stepped into the street. It didn’t signify. Escape was imperative. A voice sounded in his head: “At this moment Klaus Mann knew that turning-point was breaking-point.” He couldn’t silence the voice, rid himself of the words.

The hotel proprietor was behind the desk. Klaus attempted a casual “bonjour”.

“Monsieur Mann, excuse me. Your bill. When will you be in a position to settle it?”

“Soon, soon.”

“You will understand I can’t let it run further. You will understand that, I’m sure.”

“Quite, quite, I’m waiting for money that’s overdue myself… I’m on my way to the post office even now.”

Where Mielein’s monthly money-order might have arrived, or not.

As he hurried to the door, he knocked against a little table and caught his reflection in the glass above it. He looked like a madman.

The rain was almost a relief, but he hadn't gone a hundred metres before his thin suit was soaked and he was shivering. He turned into a bar, ordered a hot grog, and pressed himself against the wall. When the waiter brought his drink, he found he required both hands to lift it to his mouth. It couldn't go on, he didn't want it to go on, and yet...

A tall boy wearing a yellow shirt and washed-out blue shorts came into the bar and shook the water from his blond hair. He laughed and the dark room was brightened. He ordered a beer, and leant against the bar, his left leg straight, the other bent. They were what the Magician would have called "Hermes legs" and in these sexy eye-holding shorts... He turned into profile, looked about him and came over to Klaus's table.

"Do you speak English?"

"Yes."

"Do you object if I join you? Is it permitted?"

He spoke with an accent, Swedish perhaps. Getting neither assent nor refusal, he pulled out a chair and sat down. Blond hairs lay flat on his damp thigh.

"I didn't think France would be like this. I didn't think it would be wet on the Riviera."

He couldn't pronounce the "th" sound.

Klaus smiled.

"It's a terrible season," he said.

The boy had a snub nose and wide mouth. There were pale freckles on the lines of his cheek-bones. He looked like Willi and Klaus felt a surge of tenderness.

The boy began to speak. He had no French, he explained, and hadn't had anyone to talk to for days. He was travelling, but it got lonesome without a companion. All the same it was great to see the world. He went on in this vein. Klaus didn't listen to the words, but only to the lilting music of the voice.

"I'm not incommoding you, am I?" the boy said, flushing.

It was a word from a dictionary, incommoding.

"Not at all."

"I was with my girl, you see, but we quarrelled and she walked out on me. Too bad. Actually I'd had enough of her, we'd had enough of each other, do you understand?"

"I understand."

"Are you American?" the boy said. "You look American."

There was eagerness in his voice.

"I don't know," Klaus said. "I'm an American citizen, but before that I was German. I think you're Swedish perhaps."

"Yes indeed, that's smart of you, I am Swedish. My father admired the Germans, even the Nazis, he hoped we would enter the war on their side. Crazy, yes? But me, I prefer Americans. I really want to go to New York. And California. Do you know California?"

"A bit."

The boy ran his wet finger round the rim of his glass which emitted a little squeak, like a mouse caught by its paw in a trap.

"The thing is," the boy said, "she went off with most of our money. I'm not complaining, it was mostly hers to begin with. Her father's a big industrialist, mine's only a policeman. But," he hesitated and his knee jumped up and down in a little tremor, "it's left me in a fix. Is that right? In a fix, meaning difficulties?"

He pulled out a handful of crumpled franc notes.

"That's all I'm left with," he said. "I shouldn't really have bought this beer. I don't suppose you..."

Klaus wasn't surprised. He had seen it coming. Again the boy reminded him of Willi but Willi had offered himself in exchange. There would be no such offering here, he was sure of that, but the mere presence of the boy offered relief from solitude, from he wouldn't say what. He didn't know if he believed his story – it was probably false and he might be a routine chiseller, that open beautiful cat's face an asset – nevertheless...

"I don't know," he said. "Maybe. Actually I'm in the same position as you, but I was on my way to the post-office to see if any money has arrived for me. Here," he took a crumpled note from his breast pocket, "buy us another drink and then we'll see. Mine was a grog but I'll switch to whisky..."

"That's great."

The boy's face opened like a burst of sunshine.

"My name's Stefan by the way."

"Klaus."

With the drinks the boy expanded, flourished as if Klaus had indeed made him a promise which would free him from his difficulties. In a rush of words he recounted his travels – how they took the train from Paris to Orange and woke to the smell of the South, melons and open drains and new-baked bread and Gauloise cigarettes, and then made their way down the Rhone. It was here in Cannes that the quarrel had broken out, though to his mind it hadn't really been about anything.

"But that's girls," he said. "I expect you know. My mother's the same. When a woman wants a quarrel she'll always find some excuse. Least, that's what my father says.. Can we go to the post-office now, it's really good of you to accommodate me" (another dictionary expression). "I really appreciate it. Are you married, Klaus? No? Maybe it's better that way. Women tie you down, least, that's my opinion."

At the post office Klaus produced his passport. Mielein's money-order was there, sent by Western Union. Two hundred dollars. He got the equivalent in francs at what might have been a good exchange rate. The boy hovered behind him. There was also a letter from Erika. He put that in his pocket, against his heart. They stepped out into the square where the rain had stopped and a timid sun was emerging from the clouds. In a gesture too often made, he handed over a sheaf of notes without counting them. The boy had the good manners not to do so either, though Klaus was sure he was eager to. Instead he stuffed them into his pocket and rewarded him with a radiant smile. He couldn't have expected it would be so easy. That was Klaus's first sour thought, quickly amended. This was a boy for whom for a few years anyway it would always be easy.

Klaus sensed he wanted to be off. And why not? He'd got what he was after. But Klaus thought he deserved some return, even if he couldn't have the one he desired. So he said he would buy him lunch.

"When did you last have a good meal?"

The boy hesitated, then smiled again.

"That would be grand."

It was indeed as if he had natural good manners, and this was pleasing.

They walked towards the port, Klaus refraining from taking the boy by the arm. He wondered how much of his story was true, whether, as was possible, or probable, his girl was even now waiting somewhere to learn if he had been successful in his fishing expedition.

"Have you ever eaten bouillabaisse?"

"I don't even know what it is."

"Well, you should learn. You can't come to the south of France and go away without having tasted it."

Klaus picked at his. All the more for Stefan who ate as if his story of hunger might have been true. Klaus lit a cigarette and watched him. A little dribble of the soup escaped the left corner of his mouth and glistened gold on the soft skin. Klaus ordered a second bottle of Tavel.

"That was quite something," the boy said, laying his spoon down. "I haven't eaten like that since I don't know when. For ages. Were you in the war, Klaus?"

"Yes, I was in the American army."

How casually he managed to say that! How humiliating his efforts to enlist had been!

"But you were German. You said you were German."

"Yes," Klaus said. "For my sins."

The boy crumbled bread into little pellets and flicked them to the pavement where pigeons hopped sharp-eyed on them.

"Did you see much fighting?"

"No, I was in intelligence and then propaganda."

"But would you have shot at a German, your own countryman?"

"I don't know but I was never required to."

"My mother's a pacifist," the boy said, "except in the home. She says war's not only wrong but unnecessary."

"This one was necessary."

He took hold of the bottle and poured them each another glass.

"I'm sometimes ashamed that Sweden was neutral."

"You've no reason to be. You're how old?"

"Nineteen."

"So you were only a child."

"Yes, I was only a child."

Silence stretched between them, like a frontier protected with barbed wire. They had nothing more to say because what Klaus wanted to say couldn't be said to this boy, and the boy himself was peering at a territory so foreign that it left him without words. Besides he was keen to be off – to count the notes he had thrust into his pocket, to act on his good fortune and resume his freedom. Klaus paid the bill. They stood up. The boy held out his hand. Klaus took it and leaned forward and kissed him lightly on the cheek – more daring than the Magician with his Klaus, but as self-denying.

"Look after yourself," he said, having no doubt that the boy would. "Where will you go now?"

"Where my feet take me. And thank you. Thank you so much..."

Tank you so much. Klaus watched him loosely walk away. When he was perhaps twenty metres distant he turned and raised a hand in salute. Klaus made a small gesture in response. He imagined the boy meeting his girl at their appointed rendez-vous and saying, "I've struck lucky. There was this sad old queer, see, I felt him watching me and so... No, of course I didn't."

Well, it might not be like that. He might even have been telling the truth about their quarrel. Didn't matter either way. Klaus was grateful to him for helping him through a few hours. And now he had Erika's letter waiting for him. But first he would find a dark and quiet bar...

Erika wrote:

> Klauschen darling,
>
> You think I've deserted you and complain that we are not as one with each other as we were. But you are always in my heart. Believe that, please. You must. If you lose trust in our love, and in the love that Mielein and the Magician have for you, then what is there to stop you from surrendering to despair? We are no longer bound together by the political struggle, but we are still what we always were to each other. As for the political struggle, I know that with victory something has been taken away from you. That struggle seemed your self-justification. You were able to say that whatever else went wrong in your life, it gave you a purpose.
>
> And now you feel lost because we came through victorious and what you called correctly "the Brown

Plague" has been vanquished. Utterly, so that it may seem almost as if it never was.

I understand the feeling, for success has its own emptiness. All the same, my dear, you must also see that it's absurd to feel bereft because you no longer have the Nazis to fight against.

It is time to move on.

And then you say that you can no longer work as you used to, and this terrifies you. You are afraid that your talent is dead. But I tell you it is only sleeping. And if it is damaged it is because of the reasons which you know and these reasons offer you a new battle: to come through, to defeat your addiction.

I don't want to say much about your, to me, so sad illness – for that is what it is – an illness, a disease. Only that I pray to all available gods, whatever or whoever they may be, for you to stop this cruel game you play with yourself, which is so damaging, and to be stable. You are afraid you can't write and you behave in such a way as to make it difficult – I won't say impossible – to do so.

So your novel is stuck. You say it's moribund. But why is that? It's not that you are not capable of writing as well as you used to, but that you make it so difficult.

Oh probably you have been taking tuna or those beastly sleeping-pills, chewing them up without interruption and in desperation, and they fuddle your brain... They reduce you and leave you sulky, even sullen, and then, because the writing is not popping out, like a bullet from a pistol, you tell yourself it's not working and will never work again, and this reduces you ever so much more.

Oh if only I couldn't picture this exactly!

But if you can't write as you wish to, it's because by your own actions you make it impossible to do so.

Don't think I don't understand the temptation to despair. I have never been there myself, but since I am so close to you, part of you really, as you know I have always been, I understand it precisely

We fly to Sweden tomorrow where the Magician is to lecture, and then we go to the Netherlands where I shall see your publisher and urge him to do as you wish. And then I shall be with you. So hold on, my dear.

Despair is unworthy of you. There: I've said it.

I send you all my love,

Erika, as ever.

The letter made him weep. There was so much truth in it, and it came so near to understanding him, and yet even Erika could not do that now. Could not, in part, because the words at the end were false. He no longer had all her love; she had transferred that to the Magician, to whom despair had always been foreign.

He dried his eyes, gestured the waiter and asked for another whisky.

"A very big one, please."

He lit a cigarette. Lucky Strike? Could he still hope for one? Perhaps if *Mephisto* did at last come out in Germany? Would that make a difference, allow him to recover hope?

When he had drunk the whisky he wandered out of the bar, into the late afternoon streets, where people were happy, and walked through the streets, hoping absurdly that he might again encounter the Swedish boy. But of course he didn't.

XII

He admired the USA, but it baffled him: its immensity, its vast indifference, its solipsism. He could never be other than an exile there. New York was different, he loved New York. If he could have been happy anywhere, it would have been in New York. Once, when returning from travels to the Bedford Hotel, he had hesitated when required to list his permanent address in the register, and the sympathetic clerk had smiled and said, "After all, Mr Mann, this is your home now, isn't it?"

It could never be that, but it was nearer to being that than anywhere else then or since.

The contrasts in his life: lunch at the White House with FDR and Mrs Roosevelt – picking up rough boys in Times Square or Central Park, the line too long, most of them nameless.

He was disordered in those days, but not like now. He turned over in bed, impossible to rest, stop his mind racing, his nerves twitching.

Another Luminal. Better take two.

There was still Tomski then, but in America Tomski was more complicated than in Europe. Meeting his parents again and not being understood, living a lie to them. The sun had gone out of his smile. Klaus still loved him but they were no longer easy together. "Why should I be faithful," he asked, "when you aren't?" Klaus had no answer except tears. Political divisions too: Tomski railed against Roosevelt and conscription. In a moment of passion he would exclaim that America had nothing to do with Europe, should steer clear of its corruption. When Klaus explained patiently that… oh, he couldn't now be bothered to rehearse the arguments he had made so often and so vehemently, and which utterly failed to convince. But even in their worst quarrels, of which there were too many, something of tenderness remained.

Tenderness too with the little Russian, Ury, who looked like a faun, but was ultimately boring...

Bombs were falling on London and Erika, armed with her British passport, went there to report. Klaus feared for her safety, admired her work, knew it pulled them further apart, for while she grew stronger, he felt himself to be more and more feeble, useless indeed.

What was the fate of exiles? To write things that invited the reply, "What's that got to do with us?"

You can't go home anymore. A hotel is a parody of home. Even the Bedford.

Sleep impossible. He was shaking again. When he poured himself a whisky the bottle rattled like a prisoner's chains against the glass, which he held in both hands, for security, as he leant on the windowsill looking out on the rain with the smell of wet leaves rising towards him. Had the Swedish boy taken a train? Was he lying with his girl or trawling the bars? Absurd thoughts, he would never see him again.

He had scarcely ever even in New York or in California – where last year he had indeed yielded to the temptation of suicide but failed in that too – been so bad as he was now. He had had enough of life as never before. He longed for death as a parched man for a glass of water.

But not yet, perhaps not yet.

The failure of *Decision* had killed something in him: the superfluous Klaus.

His hopes had been so high. This time he would make a difference. It hadn't blown up in his face, more simply and humiliatingly it had expired like a pricked balloon.

He swallowed a mouthful of whisky, which tore at his throat and made him retch. Was another old friend abandoning him?

Somewhere in the distance a dog howled. Poor dog, shut out from the hearth where it would have slumbered in peace!

As a child he had dreamed often of a pale man who invaded his room. Sometimes he carried his head under his arm as if it had been a flowerpot. The disconnected head grinned at him, horribly, as if to say, "This is me, someday it will be you." It got to the stage that Klaus was afraid to sleep and it was then that his father was informed of the horror.

"Just don't look at him next time he comes," he said, "and tell him a child's bedroom is no place for a ghost. If he still hangs about, say that your father has a sharp temper and doesn't care to have ghosts in his house. That'll make him disappear, for it's well known in ghostly circles that I can make myself exceedingly unpleasant..."

Amazingly this worked. The ghost departed, never to return. It was on account of this incident that they began to call Father the Magician.

Klaus thought; as long as there remains something that makes you smile...

He had been happy as a child. He was sure of that. And he had been happy, or at least contented, in the army where in a sense he was a child again. But what an effort it had been to be accepted! He was, it seemed, an object of suspicion, subject to investigation by the FBI: as suspected leftist and homosexual. He rebutted the first allegation and, to his shame, denied the second. Flatly. Eventually his lies were, it seemed, convincing. He was called up and later received his American citizenship; it felt like a birthday present...

His comrades in the barracks found him strange. No wonder. He couldn't blame them. He was ten or a dozen years older than most, spoke with a German accent, and, in short, made no sense to them. He wrote a story about it, entitled "The Monk". Eventually, he wrote to their childhood friend Lotte Walter asking for a photograph. Because he would like to impress his comrades with a beautiful girlfriend. So send a truly seductive one with bare shoulders and bedroom eyes. She obliged and he told her that it was very peculiar to be a soldier and he couldn't explain it. He put the photograph by his bed and kissed it before going to sleep. Not that it fooled anyone, though he never touched any of his mates in the barracks, however much in a couple of cases he longed to do so.

Another whisky, another pill, even though there were hints of dawn. The poor dog still howling. It's me.

When at last he received the order for overseas, the Magician and Mielein and Erika came by train to Kansas City to see him off. The Magician embraced him, as never before. Mielein wept. Erika's mouth twitched as she said, "We'll meet on the other side." The other side: after the war is over.

In Naples, the second day, he came under fire and was glad of it. Now I am like the others.

He lay down on the bed. He had again been almost happy in Naples where he was assigned to the newspaper the *Stars and Stripes*, and spent off-duty hours in the Galleria, cruising with his eyes only, determined to do nothing which might be a blot on his army record. "We'll meet on the other side."

I don't want to survive this year. I am nearly on that other side. He closed his eyes, and this time, the whisky and the pills combined to invite sleep.

XIII

He woke sweating and afraid: a horrible dream. Gustaf in SS uniform and highly waxed gleaming boots. He brandished a riding-crop. "This time it is I who plays the role of Princess Tebab with which you insulted me and made me appear ridiculous," he yelled, and lashed out at Klaus. The first blow caught him across the face and he fell to his knees. Shrieking obscenities, Gustaf struck out again and again. The whip bit into Klaus's flesh. He smelled his own blood. "Admit you deserve it," Gustaf cried. "Confess you have wronged me." But Klaus found no words, only sobs. Then Gustaf was on his knees beside him, thrusting his face, with sulphurous breath into his. "Judas," he muttered. "Judas. I came close to loving you and you betrayed me," and began to howl.

It was still dark. Klaus felt his face wet with tears. If he had remained asleep, would they have consoled each other? "I came close to loving you" – closer perhaps than ever before or since. The thought was insupportable. How ugly, unlike Willi, Gustaf had been in that uniform!

Klaus began to weep freely, tears of exhaustion and despair. They flowed unstoppable as the river of time. "I'm at the end of everything." A shadowy shape hovered above him. He knew what it was: the ghost of an earlier night horror. He was lying on a deserted Baltic beach, stretched out on the cold wet sand while the beating of vultures' wings filled the air. "But there are no vultures in Germany," he cried out, vainly.

A cramp seized the back of his thigh. He hopped out of bed, naked, pressed his hands against his leg, stood on tiptoe to ease it. There was still some whisky in the bottle. He lifted it in both hands and swallowed. René's last words: "I am disgusted with everything."

The whisky steadied him. He tilted the bottle, this time into the glass. Why not do it now? I am being devoured by loneliness and misery. Why not escape? "But that the fear of something after death" – yet I have no fear of that. Only of life. And it's not fear, but wretchedness, boredom. He put on a dressing-gown. To die naked would be an embarrassment. The thought was amusing. He nursed the glass as a friend who had never betrayed him.

I can wait. I can still wait. I have not yet arrived at the irreversible moment. I am almost in credit here at the hotel, and the money Mielein sent me is not exhausted.

Her photograph stood in its frame on the table before him. The tenderness of her gaze without a hint even of reproach. Yes, my death would certainly hurt her. Can I be so cruel? And I still have work to do.

"Julian had thought so deeply, so often and so longingly of death that he felt it had become the shadow that accompanied him wherever he walked. Yet now, lying on the beach, listening to the murmur of the waves and smoking a cigar, he said to himself, 'Not yet, there's no urgency, I don't need anything now and that's a sort of freedom. There's only the seashore and the north breeze and the gulls crying out in the upper air, and the smoke from my cigar rising blue towards them to lose itself in the sunshine. I'm almost at ease with life. For the moment. So no need yet.' But then it came to him that this was precisely the occasion to depart. Was it possible that in the afterlife your condition might depend on the mood in which you had taken your leave of the earth and your own body? But then, was there any afterlife? Could he even conceive of such a thing? And if there was, wasn't it possible that it would be no better? That you might only exchange one form of misery and pain for another, and indeed for one from which there wasn't even the dream-possibility of release? To pass through that door and find that you have only entered another cell, with a palet bed and barred windows, and would hear the gaoler turn the key behind you?"

It was some days since he had written that and it rang horrifyingly true. What was it Erika had said? "If you can't write as you wish to, it's because by your own actions you have made it impossible to do so." But perhaps she was wrong; he was wrong too and he still could. And if so, then it was what he had made of himself, even his degeneration, that would make this novel what he intended it to be, even if for so much of the time the prose advanced haltingly like a man with his feet shackled by chains.

There was another dream he had often in which he took a cleaver and with one blow cut off his right hand. And was left with a dilemma. How then to strike off the other one?

He had come close once in New York at the Bedford. ("After all, this is your home now, Mr Mann?") He had had a quarrel with a boy called Johnny, a deserter from the American army, who had yelled reproaches and banged out in a temper. Then Tomski had telephoned to fix a rendez-vous for the next morning, and Klaus said, "Swell idea, but good-night for now." He ran a bath, hot enough to fill the room with steam, and lay in it with a little knife in his hand. He tried to open the artery on his right wrist, but the slash wasn't deep enough, there was blood but it didn't gush out, and then the knife seemed dirty as well as blunt and the enterprise the same, even stupid. He was bleeding but couldn't bring himself to cut again for a moment – afraid perhaps, shamefully afraid. He was nerving himself to make a second attempt when the telephone rang again and this time it was Chris saying, "Come out for a drink, Klaus, I'll come and fetch you." So he dried himself and tied a handkerchief round his wrist till it was red through, and then another till the bleeding stopped. In a bar off Times Square, Chris remarked the wound and said, "You mustn't be stupid, Klaus. You and me, we're not made for this sort of nonsense. We've a long time to live and suffer and besides we have work to do." So they got drunk together and Chris paid for everything. Klaus lifted the glass of whisky to him now, across the ocean and the Great Plains and in comfort in California. And the next afternoon he and Tomski had indulged in wild laughter and they hadn't quarrelled and Tomski had been affectionate as in their first days.

In bleak years of exile the Magician had called work, the Joseph novels, "his rod and his staff". "Though I walk through the valley of the shadow of death, I shall fear no evil..."

"Julian knew himself to be diminished when he thought of Anna in the concentration camp, for he was certain that she had never, even in *das Arschloch des Welt*, surrendered the will to live. And it was all the more remarkable because in the ordinary events of daily existence she had been inclined to melancholy, subject indeed to a profound depression, in which, as she had once said to him, I sit and stare at the wall and feel rats chewing at my heart. That was the way she talked, exaggeratedly, in a way which had embarrassed him, as an American, he now thought. For he had been reared with his gaze fixed on a Promised Land flowing with milk and honey. That was the American way, the future theirs to command, the Frontier with all its possibilities open to him. So how could he be so certain that Anna had defied death, refusing to hearken to its Siren call, that she had willed herself simply to go on and never surrendered that will until the moment when life was torn from her? He didn't know. Nevertheless he was certain and the thought shamed him. But you can live with shame, he told himself, indeed you may have to. That's inescapable until you break through the veil yourself. His thoughts were muddled, he knew that. Indeed to anyone else, should he ever utter them, they would make no sense. They would be the ramblings of a madman. How can you believe in her constancy, and admire it, people might say, and yet long for death yourself? It's pitiful, ridiculous. You should be ashamed of yourself. And indeed he was ashamed, ashamed because he had never been what he intended to be, perhaps what he was even intended to be. It was failure he couldn't live with, his own failure and that of the society in which he was condemned to live where everything good and noble was being tossed aside, discarded like garbage, as things that were no longer of use. So it was precisely because everything that didn't horrify him now seemed ridiculous that he was eager to be off. He wasn't proud of this feeling. It would be absurd to be proud of it. But there it was. That's how it was, how matters stood."

Klaus put his notebook down and emptied his glass. I'm obliged perhaps to go on till I can release Julian. But then there's Albert to think of too and deal with. His struggle against temptation is even more acute, more terrible, because he still seeks to believe, longs to believe, believes, despite all the evidence that is so remorselessly stacking up, in belief itself.

He looked up. To his surprise it was now day. They had got through another night.

XIV

He had slept for a bit, without dreams, and when he woke, the rain had cleared, the sky was cornflower-blue, and the sun lay on his work-table. It's possible to go on, he thought, what I wrote last night was perhaps not so bad. If I can work, really and truly work, then I can continue.

Gide had shown him two years ago a letter from an unknown young man who thanked him for having "liberated him from his upbringing in a home full of bourgeois material comfort." But he had then found himself posing the question, which he called frightening, "Free for what?" He had, as he put it, then detached himself from Gide, but had found no new masters and trembled in uncertainty. "The terrifying absurdity," he wrote, "of the Sartres and the Camuses has solved nothing and merely opens horizons of suicide..."

Immediately Klaus had wanted to meet this young man and speak with him and find a brother in him.

On the second page of the letter the young man spoke of "the confusion of all our youth" and begged for Gide to offer him "a glimmer which might indicate the direction to take... If there is a direction..."

If indeed!

"Did you reply?"

"Naturally I did. But what could I say except to urge him to submit to no creed or master, and, I said, 'Be yourself'. I haven't heard from him again. Doubtless he was disappointed by my message. After all, it's not easy to be yourself and go your own way. It's a lonely path, as you well know, Klaus. But what other is worth taking?"

Gide understood him – there was comfort there. And yet Klaus knew that Gide could never inhabit him, for he was quite certain that the old man had never wrestled with the temptation to end it all. His curiosity was insatiable. "Prodigious, really." All the same, Gide had never let him down. He was an anchor, even if the anchor's hold was loosening.

Perhaps even Julian and Albert might yet be brought to life. He wasn't finished, he told himself, drinking a *café crème* sitting outside a bar. He could do it because he was both of them. It was, sadly, a long time since he had been able to make other people seem real enough to matter. He no longer experienced the urgent need to know what others were knowing, to see, hear, feel what for a brief moment they saw, heard and felt. Time had sated his curiosity about others. Still, if he was both Julian and Albert, there were really no others in his novel, except as they encountered or remembered them, and knew alienation. And if news came – as it might any day – that *Mephisto* was at last to be published in Germany, and the German version of his autobiography also, well then...

Besides, his curiosity wasn't stone dead. That Swedish boy – he could imagine his day, even days. Perhaps he was still in Cannes. Perhaps he was on the beach. He pictured him there like Willi, stretched out on a towel, inviting admiration. He walked a little in that direction, stopping only twice for a glass of white wine; and felt better.

But of course there was no sign of the Swedish boy. He hadn't really expected him, only hoped, but hoped vaguely, without urgency, as you might elaborate in your mind the details and pleasures of a journey you would never take.

He settled himself at a café table, under a parasol, ordered a beer, to be drunk slowly, to pass the time, kill time. Relaxed, yes, truly, relaxed. Things could be worse.

Nevertheless, all my life I have been essentially second-rate... In the shade of this parasol, in the shadow of the

Magician. And my alcoholism and drug addiction... True cause, that I cannot accept life as sold to me. It was the little rat and the brown plague gave it meaning. Now, Othello's occupation's gone... Still, for the moment it's bearable. Who was it said once, no one who's met you, Klaus, ever forgets you? If only, if only... You should eat. He gestured to the waiter, ordered a sandwich, but when it came, took one mouthful and pushed it aside.

Albert... What to do with Albert? The direction was plain, but details of his daily life – how to supply them when the effort of imagination was too much for him? He consulted his notebook. Yes, he had left him in a café, drinking weak, ersatz, chicory-flavoured coffee and casting back in time, over his broken marriage. The first loss of faith when a relationship in which you have invested what seemed at the time the best of yourself simply withers. The day had arrived when Albert and his wife – what had he called her? – Hildegarde, yes, Hildegarde – she was so unreal to Klaus that he had had to leaf back thirty pages to find the name – when Albert and Hildegarde had faced each other over the supper-table and found that their dialogue had expired. And this wasn't – or wasn't entirely – because Klaus could find no words for them to speak to each other. It was also because it was the way it had to be. Albert clung to what remained of his faith in Communism and the Party because it was all that was left to him. His marriage was bare as the branches of a winter tree. And then he is summoned before one of the Party secretaries and accused of bourgeois deviationism because his last newspaper columns have been devoid of optimism. "They show no faith in the future," he is told, "and this is not permitted." Which is why Albert is now drinking this substitute for coffee and struggling to supply the Party with what is demanded of him. "You must correct your thinking," he has been told. "What use is thought if it doesn't lead to right action?" So he would have to oblige. It was his duty. But he couldn't find the words for the sentiments that were required. All his life he had been able to find words, and now he couldn't.

Klaus turned over a couple of pages. What was this?

"After supper she twiddled perfunctorily the knobs of the wireless beside Cousin Francis's chair – it had pleased him to have the war at his elbow; she was pleased to have only one more and more significant degree of silence added to the library; evidently the battery was dead..."

This wasn't part of his novel, and it took him a few minutes to remember that it was a passage he had copied out from an English novel by Elizabeth Bowen which he had been reading a few weeks ago. It was the "more and more significant degree of silence" that had appealed to him; also, "evidently the battery was dead..."

Terrible phrase: evidently the battery was dead.

But of course in Germany it hadn't been long before the post-war battery was recharged. That was the extraordinary thing! It was beyond satire!

A blue-and-white ball was kicked across the roadway and came to rest under his table. A small boy scurried after it and dived on it, knocking against Klaus's legs. He looked up, beamed a smile and a "Pardon, m'sieu..." and was off to rejoin his friends. He climbed on to the railing overlooking the beach, and sat there with the ball held in both hands. Aware of Klaus's gaze following him, he waved a hand, and then leaned forward to speak to one of his friends and they both laughed, and jumped off the railing back down to the beach. Klaus watched them run, jostling each other, to the water's edge and splash each other in the sunshine.

Yes, his life had been like that once.

It was too much. He paid for his beer and the sandwich he hadn't eaten, and turned away from the sea, back into the town, to another café in an alley which was in shadow. He took a seat at the back of the room, ordered a whisky-and-soda, and lit a cigarette.

It was astonishing how quickly the battery had been recharged. Beyond satire, certainly, though he had attempted that, when speculating how long it would be before Goering's second wife, the actress Emmy Sonnemann, was back on the Berlin stage.

"Perhaps," he'd written, "one of those gassed in Auschwitz has left a play in which this fine lady could make her comeback? For of course she will have known nothing about Auschwitz, will she? And besides, what has Art to do with Politics?" He had written these sentences with relish.

What had provoked the essay was news of Gustaf's return to the Berlin stage. He had spent some months as a prisoner of the Russians, had apparently won the favour of the camp commandant by staging a theatrical production and been released. Now he was about to test the loyalty of his public. The performance was a sell-out, well before the first night. It was with difficulty that Klaus, who had flown in fascinated curiosity to Berlin, managed to get hold of a black market ticket. It was a comedy by Carl Sternheim, set in Wilhelmine Germany. Gustaf produced it and played the lead – of course he did – what else would have been tolerable? The curtain rose to show him alone on stage, sitting at a desk, and this was met with thunderous applause that lasted at least five minutes before he was able to speak. He sat there smiling the while, and there was a comparable manifestation of enthusiasm at the final curtain, even though, Klaus thought, Gustaf hadn't actually been right for the part. What did it signify? he had wondered then and asked in the piece he wrote about the evening. He still wondered, could come to no conclusion even now, except this: no matter what he had done, who he had betrayed, how he had prostrated himself before Goering and Goebbels and the little rat, Gustaf remained the darling of Berlin, pre-Nazi, Nazi and now post-Nazi Berlin. Klaus was not only puzzled by it; he felt defeated.

But he knew what Gide would say. "Prodigieux, n'est-ce pas?" And it was indeed; truly prodigious.

He called for another whisky. It was a nice bar, a safe one, dingy, quiet, only one table occupied by blue-overalled workers playing cards and drinking red wine. He closed his eyes, content to listen to their muttered comments on the game and the occasional cry of triumph as a trick was taken. Perhaps he dozed off for a little. Then he heard the click-clack of table football and opened his eyes.

It was the Swedish boy, still in the washed-out blue shorts but now wearing a red shirt. There was a girl with him, also blonde. They were intent on the game and laughed often. Klaus watched them, wondering for a moment if they were really there or belonged to a dream. Then the boy turned and caught sight of him.

"Hey, Klaus," he cried and took the girl by the arm and brought her over to the table, saying something to her in Swedish as he did so.

"This is Ingrid," he said. "We met again and made up. Is that right? Made up?"

"It's right."

Without waiting to be asked he pulled out a chair for her and himself leaned over and shook Klaus by the hand. Then he sat down and crossed his legs, resting his right ankle on his left knee. He smiled broadly.

"It's great to see you again."

His shirt was unbuttoned to the waist and his chest was smooth and hairless, his belly flat.

Klaus beckoned to the barman and Stefan said he would have a beer and Ingrid a lemonade.

"And another whisky-soda for me," Klaus said.

The boy explained how he'd gone to the station intending to take a train to Italy because if you come south and don't go on to Italy then everyone in Sweden thinks you're crazy, really crazy, and he'd found Ingrid there sitting on her rucksack and weeping.

"So I felt a heel, like they say in the movies – that's where I get my American expressions, you know – because she was unhappy and maybe I'd been in the wrong when we quarrelled. So we made up and we're together again, and it's great. Isn't it great, honey?"

"It's OK," the girl said, "but you're right, you really were a heel."

"Ingrid reads books. She's educated, not like me. She's a student of literature. Maybe she's read some of yours, Klaus. Have you been translated into Swedish?"

"Once or twice."

"What's your name?" she said. "Stefan has just called you 'Klaus', nothing more."

"That's all I told him. We were only on first-name terms, nothing more. But it's 'Mann'."

"Mann? Did you write *Dr Faustus*?"

"No. That was my father."

"Your father? He's famous, isn't he? Won the Nobel, yes? I started reading it in German, but I got stuck. It was too difficult. Stefan said you're American. How come?"

"I used to be German," he said, and gave her a smile, "but now I'm American..."

As much as I'm anything, he thought.

The boy tried to keep the conversation going, as if he really wanted them to like each other, and also as if he was showing each off to the other. Klaus did what he could to help him. He watched the boy's mouth and the faint dampness on his cheekbones. The girl looked sulky.

"So you ran away from Germany," she said, "and didn't fight in the war?"

"Klaus was in the American army," the boy said.

"Didn't you feel some kind of a traitor when German cities were being bombed and destroyed? I've seen some of the destruction. My parents took me to Germany in '46. My mother's mother was German. She was homeless, her house in Stuttgart bombed, and we brought her home to Sweden. She was a nervous wreck. She never recovered and we had to put her in a home. It was awful."

"Yes," Klaus said, "I can see it must have been. But the Germans brought it on themselves."

"Not my grandmother," she said.

"So she was one of Hitler's victims too," he said, hoping to conciliate her, but wondering, as he always did on such occasions, how she had voted in '33.

Conversation languished. Then she said she had to go freshen up.

Klaus touched the boy's arm.

"I'm sorry," he said. "I'm afraid I've offended her."

"That's all right. She's easily offended. She's difficult. I'm not sure we've really made up. She says she doesn't know she can really trust me again."

"Why's that?"

"I don't know, do I? She's like that. Girls are, in my experience. The grandmother was a rabid Nazi, by the way. I've heard her speak with my father... The pair of them just the same. It disgusted me."

"It was easy to be a Nazi then," Klaus said. "I always knew that, though I never understood why."

When the girl came back she made it clear she wanted to be off. This time it was Stefan who leaned over and kissed Klaus on the cheek. Perhaps he did so to irritate the girl. Klaus didn't know, but the little gesture pleased him.

"Look after yourselves," he said. "Be happy. I think it's perhaps possible again to be happy."

For others anyway, he thought.

As they stepped out into the late afternoon, the boy turned and raised his hand and smiled. Klaus lifted his hand in reply. *Moriturus, te saluo.*

I'll never see him again, he thought. Yet we had a moment of intimacy. If I had met him again without the girl... might he have... pointless to think of it.

Perhaps he might give him to Albert, in the guise of a boy who should have been lost when everything he had been taught in the Hitler Youth crumbled about him, but who had been able, on account of his natural vitality, to shrug it off? And Albert might set himself to destroy him precisely because he found this vitality intolerable? Could I imagine that, he thought, I who long to be swept up in the arms of such vitality?

He remembered the two German prisoners he had interviewed in Italy in May '44. He'd called them Fritz and Peter in the article he'd written. Peter was a corporal in his thirties. He had been a schoolmaster. He had never joined the Party. "Certainly," he said, "from '33 to '41 things went pretty well. But I always thought it was a fairy-tale that would end badly. Now we can only hope that the regime collapses before Germany is utterly destroyed."

Then he'd called in Fritz, a lieutenant, aged twenty-two or -three. A handsome blond boy ashamed to have allowed himself to be taken prisoner... Twelve or so when the Nazis came to power, he had joined the Hitler Youth and revelled in it. "It was marvellous," he said, exhaustion fading from his eyes as he spoke." But then the Bolshevists and the international Jewish plutocracy forced war on Germany. "You really believe that, do you?" Klaus said.

The boy flushed. "Everyone knows it's true, everyone who has not been taken in by Jewish lies."

"And do you still believe Germany can win this war?"

"But of course, we shall win it because we have to. I admit that things are going badly just now, but that will change. There's word, you know, of a new secret weapon that is being prepared. It will change everything."

"And have you no regrets?"

"Yes, certainly, I regret that I have been taken prisoner. I would have preferred to die for the Fuehrer..."

Well, that hadn't been permitted him. He had been sent to a camp in England. And what would have become of him since, five years later? Was he still spouting the same repulsive nonsense?

Klaus hadn't been able to hate him. Indeed he had felt sorry for the boy who didn't speak what he recognised as German, only Nazi-German. Could he have been brought to see the foul absurdity of all he had been reared to believe in?

He called for another whisky-soda. It wouldn't be dark for hours yet.

Hours later in velvet night he found himself at the Zanzi Bar again. He had come there without hope of finding Miki, whose employer has decided they should sail to Corsica; but there was nowhere else and he felt hollow to the pit of his stomach. He ordered a whisky-soda. He didn't know how many he had had in the other bar after the Swedish boy walked out of his life for the second and surely last time, but it was one of those nights when he couldn't get drunk, no matter how many whiskies he downed. He had wanted that lieutenant Fritz, all the more keenly because his words were so stupid and horrible and he disgusted him and he knew he couldn't have him. And of course he had reminded him of Willi, just like the Swedish boy.

The bar was busy, full of smoke and laughter with an undercurrent of despair. There was a nice-looking sailor-boy snuggling up to a fat old Egyptian who was stroking the boy's neck. No one approached Klaus's table. I look old and ill and poor, he thought, the Egyptian stinks of money. There were rings on the fingers now pressing on the sailor's shoulder...

A man in a crumpled linen suit rose from a corner table and made for the lavatory. It was Guy Probyn. The boy at his table lifted his hand and waved towards Klaus, who recognised him as the one from the Villa Mauresque. When he saw he had caught Klaus's attention, the boy's mouth opened and his tongue flicked from side to side. Well, why not? Klaus picked up his glass and crossed the room to join him. The boy got up and offered his face for a kiss. Klaus obliged.

"I'm so glad to see you again," the boy said. "I'm Eddie, remember? I didn't dare speak to you the other day. I was afraid Willie would be jealous. He's so possessive, you can't imagine, even if it gave him pleasure that day to treat me like dirt. And I was so disappointed when you left because I wanted to tell you I really adored your *Alexander*. Willie pretends I can't read, but really and truly I read lots, and I loved, just loved, that novel. So there..."

"Sweet of you," Klaus said. "I was very young, like you, when I wrote that."

"Well, I adored it. I'm delighted to have the chance to tell you so."

Klaus was reminded of the famous critic who made a point of telling authors how much he had enjoyed and admired the first novel they had published, with the implication that they had never done anything half as good again. But this boy Eddie wasn't like that; he wanted to please Klaus and it was probable that *Alexander* was the only book of his he had read. So he didn't say, as he might have in other circumstances, "I've written better since."

Guy Probyn loomed over them.

"So you two know each other."

"We met at the Villa Mauresque," Klaus said.

"Ah yes. The old lady said you'd been to lunch, he thought you looked distressed. Talented, he said, but will he ever make anything of it? You shouldn't worry. I've heard him express the same doubts about every writer half his age. We've been banished this evening, Eddie and I. Important guests we're not grand enough to be allowed to meet. The ex-King of England and Her Royal Highness, as he insists she must be called, no less... Of course Willie has to keep up appearances in such company. It's ridiculous because it's not even as if it makes him happy. So I thought Eddie might benefit from a spot of louche life. Not that there's much in evidence here tonight..."

The boy fluttered his long dark eyelashes and looked sideways at Klaus...

"I don't mind," he said. "Willie snubs me in company, and at these grand dinners I never know which piece of cutlery to use next."

He smiled, modestly, to suggest he was an ingenu, perhaps. Actually he's a nice kid and a pretty boy and I think I could detach him from Guy and have him without much trouble, but he's not the Swedish boy whom I can't have.

"We could all do with another drink."

Later Guy Probyn said,

"I finished *Mephisto* and I haven't changed my mind. It's very good, I grant you, even brilliant, but, speaking as a friend of Gustaf, I can't but conclude that the way you treat him stinks."

Klaus felt unutterably weary. He picked up his glass.

"Perhaps because I'm no longer his friend, I can't agree with you. And perhaps also because I remain in some way German and can't forgive those who collaborated with the regime and, in Gustaf's case, licked the Fat Man's well-polished boots."

"You're harsh, Klaus, very harsh. That's why you will never be more than second-rate. You lack sympathy. Your father would have understood him as you don't. 'Brother Hitler', you know. But you divide your characters into those you like and those you don't and you can't be fair to the second lot. Princess Tebab, for instance, she's absurd, you don't begin to understand a woman like that. You can't. Ah, there's Billie. Excuse me while I have a word with the slut."

He clapped Klaus on the shoulder as if he was a comrade to whom he was entitled to speak sharply...

"He doesn't like you, does he?" the boy said.

"Not a lot, it seems."

"I don't much like him myself."

He took hold of Klaus's hand and pressed it on his own thigh.

"Yes?" he said.

"No," he said, "no, not tonight anyway. I'm old and tired and a little drunk."

"But you like me? Another time? You know where to find me."

"That might be difficult."

"Don't worry, I'd find a way."

He leaned over and kissed Klaus on the lips, very softly.

"See?" he said. "We could have fun. We would have fun. That book he was running down, I'd like to read it. Mr Maugham pretends I can't read, but I read a lot."

Klaus felt tears prick his eyes, but he mustn't weep, not here, where Guy Probyn might think he was the cause. And it wasn't like that. It was like he didn't know what. You can't go home again, and this boy... who, aware that Guy was coming back, had gently returned him his hand.

"Time we were off, young fellow. The curfew tolls the knell of parting day. I promised Alan I'd get you back for beddy-byes. The old lady's a stickler for punctuality, as you know, and their Royal Highnesses will have bored him silly, so he'll be in a vile temper if you're late. Good seeing you, Klaus. Hope the present work's going well."

He swept the boy away, but, as they reached the door, Eddie turned and smiled and again flicked his tongue from side to side. Klaus beckoned to the barboy, and asked for another whisky-soda.

"A very very large one."

Billie shimmied to his table, pulled out a chair and sat down.

"Buy me a drink, will you, please. You're a friend of Miki, aren't you. He's a good friend of mine too. That Monsieur Probyn, he's a piece of shit. The things he said to me. He's no right to speak to me like that, just because he has rented me a couple of times."

The barboy brought Klaus his whisky-soda in a large tumbler and looked enquiringly at Billie.

"Please buy me a drink, " he said, "I really need it and I'm skint."

"Why not?" Klaus said. "The same for this gentleman."

Billie giggled.

"Gentleman?" he said, "you're a sport, you really are. Gentleman, that's not the description I usually get. Take me home with you later?"

Klaus shook his head.

"I'm not in the mood. So drink your whisky. You're quite right about Monsieur Probyn, though, you've got him nicely summed up."

XV

Klaus woke with words in his head. What do men want from me? Why do they pursue me? Why are they so hard on me? All I am is a perfectly ordinary actor...

A perfectly ordinary actor... They were the final words he had given to Hendrik who was Gustaf, the last sentence of *Mephisto*. Didn't this howl of puzzled indignation do him justice, whatever Guy Probyn thought? And wouldn't Gustaf, if he had truly read the novel, have realised that, despite everything, Klaus understood that his ambition and egotism had driven him into a wasteland of despair? Wasn't there sympathy in these last words?

In a sense he had written them despite himself, despite his resentment and the contempt he had felt. Brother Hendrik, Brother Gustaf...

He was curiously serene, as if he found himself on dry land after danger of drowning and experiencing the most violent sea-sickness. Washed out, but serene. Yes it was indeed strange, "prodigious really".

The sun was shining, as if it too was surprised to be free of clouds.

"Albert," he wrote, "knew a moment of lucidity: you didn't have to believe in the future to endure the present. He turned over another card. It was just possible that this time his game of Patience would work out. Black two on Red three."

Strange: he hadn't thought that Albert would have a moment of something that felt almost like hope. Well, how would he feel when Klaus returned to him next?

It was time to dress. He had a lunch engagement. Doris, a friend since their youth, was one of the few people, not counting family and boys, with whom he could still bear to spend time. He didn't have to wear a mask for her. She always knew how bad things were with him.

"OK, Klaus," she would say, "the avalanche is descending, the floor's about to give way, nevertheless, we've survived worse."

And she would make him laugh: extraordinary.

He ran a comb through his hair, what was left of it. How miserable he had been when the first signs of baldness appeared. And now it didn't matter.

In the streets people exchanged smiles with each other, all on account of the sun, there might still be something of even this miserable spring to be salvaged. A ginger cat basking on a wall allowed him to scratch it behind the ear, and purred warmly. In the middle of a little square half a dozen small boys were kicking a football and crowing with what must be happiness, animal pleasure in simply being. From an open window came the sound of music he paused to listen. A song he knew. Charles Trenet, "Bonsoir, jolie madame." The effortless line of the melody. Even the policemen looked happy.

Doris was late. She was always late. It was her one selfishness. It was, he knew, because she hated to be kept waiting herself. It frayed her nerves, she had said, often. "I can't help it, it's stronger than I am," she would excuse herself.

He took a seat at a corner table on the terrace by an oleander bush. The waiter, old enough to be his father, his waistcoat spotted with stains no cleaning could remove, brushed invisible crumbs from the pink tablecloth. Klaus asked for a gin-and-Dubonnet. He didn't know why. It was something he hadn't drunk for years. But it was all right. It was – almost – as if everything was all right.

Here she was, only ten minutes late. They embraced.

"What's that you're drinking, darling?"

"Gin-and-Dubonnet."

"What a good idea!"

"How was Paris?"

"Wet."

"It's been wet here, raining for days. Now you're back, the sun's come out."

"Flatterer. How have you been?"

Klaus gestured vaguely, as if shrugging his shoulders would be too much trouble.

"You look better," she said. "In fact, you look good. The clinic obviously worked."

"I suppose so – if it's obvious, it must have."

"All the same, Paris was, well, Paris. I walked in the Luxembourg, went to exhibitions, not that the new painters are much good. Oh, and I did as you asked, went to the Tournon and had a drink for Roth."

"Thank you," he said. "I think of him often, you know."

"Yes, Poor man."

On another day he might have replied, "Poor both of us," but now he smiled and took hold of her hand.

The waiter brought the menu. They ordered an omelette, to be followed by red mullet, grilled with tarragon.

"And frites," Doris said. "I know I'm too fat. Nevertheless..."

"Frites it is then," Klaus said.

It was extraordinary. He was hungry. He had an appetite.

"And a bottle of Tavel," he said.

Because the sun was shining? Because he had drunk it with the Swedish boy?

"Have you met anyone nice?" she said. "That's what you really need, Klaus. Someone nice to be in love with. Then you could forget all the nonsense."

The dribble of soup which had escaped the boy's mouth and glistened gold between his lower lip and chin.

"You read my thoughts," he said. "But there's no one."

"Never mind," she said, "we've got each other."

"So you're not in love either?"

"I'm always in love," she said, "and it's always hopeless. This one says she truly loves her husband. Imagine that," she laughed.

"What a pair of failures we are!"

"But we've got each other."

"So we have."

After the fish, they had a salad, and then a flan. They drank coffee and Doris had a Cointreau and Klaus an Armagnac. Then they strolled to the public garden and sat on a bench and Doris put her arm around him and said, "Let's play at journeys. Where shall we go?"

"North Africa," he said, "Marrakesh."

"That's good. We can get a boat from Marseille."

When, later, they parted, Doris saying, "She's agreed to meet me this afternoon because her husband's away on business," Klaus remained on the bench, smoking. He sat there for a long time as afternoon turned to evening, at peace with himself, remembering the sweetness of youth, walks by the Isar or the Neckar, picnics in the park, the unfolding of innumerable possible futures. He smiled to think of the curiously innocent corruptions of Berlin in the Weimar years when even wickedness was a sort of play-acting – innocent corruptions, certainly, in view of the dank corruption of the spirit which succeeded them. The sweetness of south German life – he could almost taste it again.

Yet innocence is always dangerous, he thought now. There was a story he had written when he was very young, it was about that attractive mystery boy called Kaspar Hauser, a tale more than a hundred years old. He was dumb and timid and utterly ignorant and guileless, for he had spent the first sixteen years of his life imprisoned in a dark cave, and learned to speak, but then only haltingly, in the year after his release. All sorts of stories were told to account for him. According to one he was a prince who had been buried alive by jealous relatives. But others said he was an impostor, and others a half-wit. No one knew. Then, within only a few years of his release, he was found murdered, which, Klaus thought when he wrote the story, seemed to support the theory that he was indeed of royal blood. His cruel fate appealed to poets, who made him a symbol or rather the incarnation of melancholy and innocence... Klaus's story had been a poor one. He couldn't rise to the theme. But the thought of poor speechless Kaspar accompanied him for years, and now he seemed to symbolise for him that "other Germany" of which he and Erika had dreamed and written. Like Kaspar it had been thrust into a dark cave in the Brown Years and left to rot; now, set free, would it recover speech? Or would it be murdered, crushed between the Red East and a renascent Fascism, supported by the USA? And wasn't the reception given to Gustaf on his return to the Berlin stage proof that this Kaspar, the "other Germany", had not recovered the power of speech?

Perhaps he might write his story again; better this time. But no: you can't go home again. You may revisit the past in memory, but you can't live there.

There was mail for him at the hotel. Three letters. The proprietor handed them over with what was almost a smile, Klaus being more or less in credit.

"Good news, I trust," he said.

He means money, Klaus thought, thanked him, mounted the stairs, slowly on account of a dull pain in his left calf, and unlocked the door of his room. It was cool and dark, and when he switched on the light it flickered two or three times before glowing dully. He dropped the letters on the table, and took his reserve bottle of Johnnie Walker from the clothes cupboard. He poured himself a big drink and added only a brief splash of soda.

He opened the one with an Italian stamp first. It was from Rossellini. Sorry, regrets, good of you to have put the proposition to me, but it's not for me. A nice idea, nice outline, the pages of script offered possibilities, but for some other director. He was, cordially, his friend.

No surprise. He hadn't really expected anything of Rossellini, who in any case had deprived him of a credit for the film for which he had written the first draft in the year after the war. He had liked him, but hadn't enjoyed the experience of working with him, and in any case he had never believed, only hoped, that this idea for a film based on these two German prisoners-of-war was his sort of thing.

So he laid the letter aside and picked up the one with a Dutch stamp. Hirsch, his support for years, was also sorry. There were no royalty payments due, and, as for a loan in the form of another advance, what could be offered was almost contemptible, he was ashamed to write. Nobody valued Klaus more highly than he, or set a greater store on his friendship, but times were tough, his own business was in trouble, Klaus would understand how it was. Meanwhile, dear friend, finish your novel which I look forward to with eagerness and a lively curiosity…

Finish the novel? It was going nowhere. Every sentence he wrote led him further into a morass from which he could see no way out. That too was how it was, even when, as this morning, the sentences seemed good. He gave himself another whisky and hesitated before opening the last letter from the publisher in Berlin who had been enthusiastic about bringing out new German editions of *Mephisto* and his autobiography.

Did he dare? Should he thrust it into Kaspar's dark cave?

The laughter of children in the street rose to him, happily. Hs slid his thumb under the flap.

It couldn't have been worse. The books were marvellous, as Klaus himself knew. It would have been an honour to publish them. But it was impossible. A letter from Gustaf Gründgens' lawyers threatened legal action if the publication went ahead. Their client has been slandered and would demand substantial damages. Meanwhile they were in any case considering whether there were grounds for an injunction prohibiting publication. I can't afford to fight such an action, Klaus, and neither can you, can you? Klaus must realise that Gustaf's popularity was enormous, and his power consequently great. It would do me great harm to be seen to slander him. So, with many regrets, he must abandon the intention to publish. Fortunately no contract had been signed. Perhaps some other publisher would be prepared to bear the costs and endure the obloquy. But for him it was impossible. Klaus would understand. He remained of course his friend and admirer.

There was a postscript, hand-written.

"Write something else, Klaus, and let me have it. A light novel now, about your youth in Munich perhaps.There's already a nostalgia for those days. People look for diversion in these difficult times. Give me a comedy and I shall be delighted to publish it. But, please, no hint of Gustaf Gründgens... It's simply impossible."

Impossible. Everything was impossible, absurd. The children's laughter still rose to him, but when dark fell that poor dog would howl again.

Klaus opened his notebook. On the First of January he had written, "I don't wish to survive this year." Now the door out was open to him.

"Mielein," he scribbled, "Erika", and had nothing to add.

That was it.

He had nothing, truly nothing.

He must leave Julian and Albert to their fate, No one was interested, nobody.

The ultimate absurdity would be to go on.

A light novel... He unscrewed a pill bottle, poured a handful and thrust them into his mouth. A swig of whisky, Johnnie to the rescue, but rescue was escape. The bottle was not yet half-empty.Help me on my way, Johnnie. He lay down on the bed, stretched out his hand for another drink. And another. More pills to be sure of passing from the absurd into... what? Nothingness, please, nothingness... The image of the Swedish boy floated before him. But he was already on the other side of the frontier, and a Border guard examined Klaus's passport and said, "This is out of order." He carried it off – "Confiscated, mein Herr" – and beyond the barbed wire the Swedish boy lifted his hand in farewell and turned away towards the light.

He opened his eyes. "Evidently the battery is dead."

Another drink, and another, and he began to drift away.

Mielein, Erika, forgive me. I can't go on... You can't go home again, not to the little Princess and the boy in the sailor suit, not anymore. There is no home to return to... This time, please, let me go...

Other Stories

Forbes at the Festival

Adam Forbes, a Scots writer, unable for reasons he had never defined to live in Scotland, or indeed to write much, was an unlikely person to have been invited to speak about Scottish literature at a Festival – itself equally improbable – held in a small town in the Tuscan Maremma. He had never heard of the town, and the region, which he didn't know, was associated in his mind with a shaggy white sheepdog and with a book – a novel? short stories? essays? – by Ouida. He had never read it, but could picture where it had stood, brown-covered, on a shelf in his second wife's bedroom. It might still be there, though it was he, not Arabella, who had bought it.

He was older, some way older, than the other participants in the Festival, except for a Sicilian novelist, said to be famous. Forbes himself, if never that, had once been well known, quite well known anyway, in certain circles, small circles admittedly. But that was a long time ago. So the invitation had come as a surprise. He kept getting the name of the town wrong. Like so many things now. His Italian had once been fluent, if never grammatically correct. Sad to find that, like his linen suit, it was worn out. There were holes in the jacket pockets and holes in his memory. For instance: that girl met one afternoon long ago in the Borghese Gardens, just by the entrance to the Zoo. They had gone back to his hot dark room in a *pensione* in the Piazza dei Santi Apostoli and made love – "had sex", he thought they would say now. He had forgotten her name and the colour of her hair, but he could picture her arms, rounded, smooth and glowing in the sunshine of the garden. But how to describe them? There's no comparison that is right for the colour of skin, it's a question, he thought, of texture. If that girl returned to him now it was because of the beauty of the waitress last night at the restaurant in the little square in front of the church. Yet probably there was no real resemblance, beauty all that they shared. He had thought it would be the beginning of an affair when she gave herself to him – eagerly? yes, certainly eagerly – but when she slipped on her knickers and he put the question you always put, "No way, my father flies in tonight and then we are off to Greece before we go home to Seattle." As for the waitress with her proud Renaissance beauty and her dark-bronzed skin which made him wonder if she had Arab blood – or Jewish or Gypsy? – she was seventeen at most, and Forbes was in his sixty-third year and alert to murmurs of mortality.

He sat at a table outside a café, fanned his face with his straw hat and lit a cigar. There was a picture of Garibaldi on the packet, and this was appropriate, for the festival sessions were being held in a salon of the municipality in the neighbouring square which was indeed the Piazza Garibaldi. The back of the packet informed him that "L'Eroe dei due mondi è stato un grande fumatore di sigari, naturalmente Toscani..." As for the cigars themselves, it was pleasant to learn that they had been "accuramente selezionati per ottenere un gusto morbido, pur nella costanza della tradizione tipica ed inimitable, più dolce e raffinato." Just what you aimed for in writing, the accurate selection of words to create certain effects, and the words were well chosen in this advertisement – even if, he reminded himself, *morbido* was what his French-English dictionary called a *faux ami*, the Italian meaning soft or delicate, the English 'morbid' being translated by *morboso.* No matter: the thought that he enjoyed the same brand of cigar as the hero of two worlds was oddly pleasing. "Il fumo," another notice drafted by a less sympathetic hand informed him "provoca cancro mortale ai polmoni" – nothing *raffinato* or *dolce* about that message. Nevertheless he drew deeply on his cigar.

Every cigar or cigarette had become a small act of defiance, not only of the threatened death, but of the world he had survived into. Smoking was no longer only what a biographer of Thomas Mann had called it: the drug of those who are ready to go along with the middle-class game but need compensations to endure it. It was now openly oppositional, rebellion against programmed rationality. "Even if I wanted to," he would say, "I wouldn't give up now." He was aware of having become a bore on the subject.

Now, a girl appearing from inside the bar, he ordered an espresso and a grappa.

He took out a notebook which, on leaving home in Gravesend, he had stuffed into his pocket, just in case, here in Italy where indeed he had always kept and used such a book, he might think of something worth recording. It was, he now discovered, an old book, more than half used-up. He opened it at random.

"From G Robb's biog of V Hugo: 'Everyone is a lunatic in the privacy of his own mind.' That was good, but was it Robb or Hugo himself? Most probably Robb. There was nothing to add; Forbes was conscious he frequently now made little sense, even to himself. Nothing to add, except perhaps "and of course a genius", though that too is a lunatic delusion.

And, on another page, this: "All the girls I've ever written were really one girl. She was sixteen and we lay on a bank by a river while our horses grazed. She was honey-coloured and wore a short-sleeved yellow aertex shirt and dark brown jodhpurs. I leaned over and kissed her and she responded. Then when I slipped my hand inside her shirt, she wriggled away and said no. We rode back to the riding-school stable. She was a holiday girl and the next day they left. Later we exchanged letters.

Hers were always disappointing, but I refused to be disappointed. Next year at holiday-time she wasn't there and her parents told my mother she was in France on an exchange. She hadn't told me. Our correspondence withered and I never saw her again. A long time later my sister told me her marriage had broken up and she had become grotesquely fat."

What had prompted him to write that? "Honey-coloured" was vile, sloppy, since honey comes in a variety of shades. All the same, he knew what he had meant and he could still see her slightly damp skin and her wide mouth and snub nose; and, yes, he had imagined himself in love, had perhaps really been in love, first love anyway, therefore never quite dead. But the suggestion that she was all the girls he had ever written was rhetorical nonsense.

Or was it?

A few months previously, on what was now for him a rare visit to London, he had met an old school-friend Edward, with whom he had years ago talked books and writers for hours – tired the sun with talking, he now thought self-mockingly. They hadn't seen each other for years, more than twenty he was sure, but they had had lunch and then, for old time's sake, gone round to the Colony Room to drink brandy. Breaking off one of these sad "whatever became of old Archie?" conversations, Edward had said, "You know, I've had scores of boys over the years, more than I could count, and the trouble with every one of them was that they weren't Bobby Macrae;" and he had rolled the brandy round in the glass. Bobby Macrae, a blond boy who had played Puck to Edward's Oberon in a school production of the "Dream", not right for the part, Forbes remembered, being round-faced and stocky. "Can't think," someone had said, "what Edward sees in that big bum." Only too obvious really.

"And do you know," Edward said, "he lives in Australia now and is bald and the father of five daughters. Yet that doesn't matter. I had lunch with him when I went there for the Adelaide Festival. He bored me of course, nevertheless... I think I'm a little drunk."

So perhaps what Forbes had written in this notebook about Sheila, whenever, wasn't so far from being true. First loves stay with you, he thought, as no others. All the more when they come to nothing as was almost certainly the case with Edward's for Bobby Macrae.

A girl passed, slowly. She was blonde, long-legged, in a loose flowered skirt that came half-way down her calves. She wore sandals, but walked elegantly. A boy sitting sideways on his stationary scooter called out "bella". She didn't turn her head to look at him.

Forbes relit his cigar which had gone out the way Toscani do. He glanced at his watch. Almost time to go to the next session of the conference, only civil to do so; attendances had, he understood, been disappointing so far, except for the concert of Gaelic music in the castle courtyard the first evening. He paid his bill and set off, leaning on his stick. He was sweating in the afternoon heat. At least it would be cool in the fine reception room of the municipality.

He was early, the platform still unoccupied. He looked over the books laid out on a table. There was an Italian edition of a novel he had written a long time ago; he couldn't remember ever having seen it before. Still, it was something, he supposed. His own books made a poor show in comparison with the works of other speakers. There were six or seven titles from the Sicilian veteran, and a pile of a dozen or so copies of the novel by this session's speaker. He was a thirty-something Scottish writer and a card propped against the pile declared him to be the winner of a prize which Forbes had never heard of.

He really was out of things, but then he had known that for a long time and had accepted the invitation to the Festival only because it promised him a free, or more or less free, few days in Italy.

People were taking their seats, not in any great number. The chairman began her introduction, first in Italian, then English. Kyle Hutcheon, she said, had been acclaimed as the most talented of a new wave of Scottish writers. His novel, set partly in Glasgow and partly on the West Coast of America, had already been translated into half a dozen languages, including of course, she was happy to say, Italian. Kyle would be happy to sign copies after the event. Unfortunately Kyle himself didn't speak Italian, but she would translate what he had to say for the benefit of Italian-speakers without English. She smiled, invitingly. The author scowled. He began to speak in a rapid mutter. Forbes, slightly deaf, couldn't follow. The chairman's Italian version was more comprehensible.

Forbes soon stopped listening. From what he gathered the subject of the novel was incest. He didn't think he would be tempted to read it. For a little he leaned back and closed his eyes. When he opened them he was surprised to see that the blonde girl had come in and taken a seat at the end of the row in front of him. She wasn't apparently listening either, for she now took a book from the shoulder bag she had placed on the seat beside her and began to read. It might of course be the great work under discussion. Forbes couldn't see the cover.

At last it was over. People began to drift away. A handful approached the author with books to be signed. The chairman approached Forbes.

"That was good, didn't you think? It's going well, isn't it?"

"Absolutely," Forbes said. She was a nice woman after all, he had decided.

"Kyle's quite an act."

"Hard to follow," Forbes said.

"Are you all right for tomorrow?"

"Yes, but, if you don't mind I'll skip the next session this afternoon. I'm feeling a bit tired. The heat, you know. Not accustomed to it these days."

"That's all right. We'll see you at dinner then."

"Is it the same restaurant as last night?"

"No, the other one in the piazza. It's essential to move them around. For goodwill, you know. See you then. I know Kyle wants to meet you."

Forbes doubted this, nevertheless returned her smile.

Back at the bar in the other piazza, the waitress greeted him as if he was already a regular customer. He asked for a beer and lit a cigar. Late afternoon was a sad time, but he felt all right. Melancholy, yes, but still content merely to be where he was, back in Italy and in the shade of the parasol erected above the table, watching life go idly by and the sun striking pink on the tufa stone.

"You're Adam Forbes, aren't you?"

To his surprise it was the blonde addressing him. The accent was American, but he could no longer tell one American accent from another.

"Mind if I join you?"

The waitress brought him his beer, and the blonde asked for an ice cream.

"Strawberry," she said. "What's strawberry in Italian?"

"Fragola," he said, but the waitress had already understood.

The blonde took a book from her bag and placed it on the table in front of him. It was an old edition – actually the only edition – of his first novel written almost forty years ago. She opened it at the page where he had dedicated it to his mother, and pointed to words written there:

"And for Lindy, in memory of the Borghese Gardens and what came after. Love, Adam."

"Surprise you?" she said.

"An understatement."

She shook out a cigarette and held up the packet.

KIM, it said.

"My name," she said, "kind of cute to find a brand with your name on it. Sorry, I haven't introduced myself. I'm Kyle's wife, that's one reason why I'm here."

He was disappointed. The young man didn't deserve her, he was sure of that.

"You were at his session. What did you think of it?"

"I'm a bit deaf," he said. "A lot of it passed me by. Over my head perhaps."

"You want to know what I thought? I thought it stank. But that's the stage we're at."

Forbes drew on his cigar.

"I see," he said, meaning I don't, and I don't care.

"I guess you haven't read his novel either. You should. It's nasty but I have to admit it's good. It's why we're breaking up, only he doesn't know that yet, so don't split on me. I'm not embarrassing you, am I?"

She was of course, but he said, "Not at all. I hope you're doing the right thing."

A meaningless remark.

"Oh, I know I am."

The girl brought the ice cream. She took a big spoonful and held it, spoon and all, in her mouth. She tapped Forbes's novel.

"So tell me about Lindy. And the Borghese Gardens. That's in Rome, isn't it?"

Lindy? The name meant nothing to him. But the Borghese Gardens and what came after? It was, surely, an absurd coincidence. "No way, my father's flying in tonight..." They were sky-blue knickers, he remembered, noonday Roman sky-blue. Had that all but explicit inscription embarrassed her? He picked up the book which had meant so much to him when he was writing it, and only a little less on the day of publication, and now had nothing to do with him. He hadn't seen it in twenty years, he told her. Where had she found it?

"I brought it with me," she said. "I made sure to bring it with me when I saw your name on the programme. So tell me about Lindy and the Gardens and what happened after. I hope you don't think me rude or importunate."

He did actually, but then he liked her for bringing out the word "importunate", which belonged to an earlier, more decorous century, and she was really very pretty.

"It's a long time ago. I'd forgotten she was called Lindy."

Maybe, he thought, I didn't know her name till I came to give her the book and write in it.

"She came from Seattle, "he said.

"I know that. Go on. Please…"

"It's difficult," he said.

"You fucked her, didn't you? That's what 'came after', isn't it."

"It was a long time ago," he said again, and drew deeply on his cigar which was on the point of going out. "Why are you interested?"

She didn't answer, but took another spoonful of her ice. She really was very pretty… "Si jeunesse savait, si vieillesse pouvait," he thought.

"I'm not embarrassing you, am I?" she said. "But it's all connected, that's what's so strange."

"I'm sorry, I don't follow."

He experienced a sudden hope that she had read that old novel, not merely its dedication. A ridiculous hope. What could it matter if she had? But one of the last things to die is an author's vanity. And if she had, might he not inscribe it to her in turn? "And to Kim also, years later." But – again – nothing of what had happened that long-distant hot afternoon could happen again now.

"Lindy was my mother," she said. "I should have started with that. She remembered you. Even in the Home she remembered you, and kept this book by her, as if… as if I don't know what."

What could he say?

"You speak of her in the past tense."

"Oh sure. She was happy to go. It was maybe the first thing she'd been happy to do in years. It was Kyle killed her. In a way. That's why I've made up my mind to leave him. Or not him precisely, but his book. You haven't read it, have you? You should. It's her story."

Hadn't someone said it was about incest? "My father flies in tonight, and then we're off to Greece before we go home to Seattle…" There hadn't been anything ominous in the words.

"She used to talk to Kyle. He can be a good listener when there's something in it for him. She gave him her ruined life and he made use of it. That's what I can't forgive him for."

He wanted to say: it's what we do. He thought of Edward and Bobby Macrae and a novel Edward had written which they hadn't talked about that afternoon in the Colony Room. Now he wondered if Edward had given the bald man with five daughters a copy of that book when they met after so many years in Adelaide. Probably not. Edward was malicious only on paper, not in everyday life.

"Would you like a drink?" he said, and when she nodded, beckoned to the waitress and ordered a campari-soda for her and a grappa and espresso for himself.

"She married," the girl said. "Married my father but she couldn't get away from her one. Do you understand? And Kyle took my father's role in his novel – the sympathetic boy from Glasgow – and told how the marriage foundered – 'got fucked' he says, 'foundered' is my word – because of how she was trapped. I don't know if she told him directly or if he divined it but he uncovered her shame – that's how the Bible put it, isn't it – uncovered it to the world, and she couldn't live with that. She'd been emotionally fragile for a long time, but now she couldn't cope with life anymore. How do you remember her?"

He couldn't say: "only her arms and her sky-blue knickers" – and the decisive way she zipped up what he had hoped – hadn't he? – might be more than it was.

Or that he hadn't thought of her in years, not till last night when that dark young beauty had smiled at him as she took his order and somehow, for no reason he could be sure of, jolted his memory.

"It was only one afternoon," he said and told her how she had asked directions outside the zoo – this itself a sudden stab of memory – and how he had gone with her to the American Express offices in Piazza di Spagna, and then, after a glass of wine and chicken sandwiches and a granita and coffee in the Caffè Greco, back to his room.

"She was sweet," he said, "and I think she was happy."

It sounded to him as if he was excusing himself. She hadn't been a virgin, he remembered that, but she wasn't a tramp either, he was sure of that, a nice girl really.

"She was always sweet," the girl said, "but not often happy."

Which of us is? he almost said, but that would have been the lunatic in the privacy of his mind speaking. There were always happy days, or at least moments in days. Curiously this was one.

"Kyle makes him out to be a monster, my grandfather I mean. I never knew him, but I've read his diaries which Kyle found in Lindy's desk when we cleared her apartment after she went into the Home. I don't think he abused her, physically I mean. But he couldn't let her go.

Kyle decided different. I can't forgive him. Do you mind that I'm telling you this? Does it embarrass you?" she asked again.

We're thieves, he thought of saying, scavengers, you can't trust us, that's what both my wives discovered, so they left me. My first, Hildegarde, was German: what did daddy do in the war? He'd written an answer to that question. He felt a surge of empathy with Kyle, though he had taken a scunner at him, and felt tenderness for this bruised girl who sipped her campari-soda and looked fragile. He would have liked to take her in his arms and kiss her, but Kyle, he knew, was a sort of brother. Strange discomfort afforded by the profession.

Two middle-aged ladies in tight-fitting dresses were eating cakes at the next table. Fragments of their conversation drifted in Forbes's direction. A long complaining story: "dunque", said one, forking cake into her mouth, "e poi," she added as if to deter interruption. What, Forbes gathered, was she to do with her son-in-law who refused to work? – all positions offered an offence to his dignity. Or had he got it wrong, with his deafness and patchy Italian?

"I shouldn't have burdened you with this," Kim said. "I'm sorry, but I did want you to know that she kept your book with her right to the end, and it mattered to her. That's why it matters to me now, in a different way."

"And your husbands's? Kyle's? That matters too."

"Yes," she said. "It's abuse, you see. You do understand that it really is abuse, don't you?"

It's what we do, he thought again of saying, and might indeed have said so this time, but he looked up and saw her husband, Kyle, turning into the piazza. She saw him too and put Forbes's novel back in her bag.

"I haven't spoken to you about this," she said. "About any of it."

He tipped his grappa into his coffee and drank it.

"This is Adam Forbes," she said to her husband.

"That was fucking pathetic," the young novelist said. "If they're going to drag you half-way across the world, you'd think they'd make sure there was an audience. Fucking waste of time."

Forbes put a match to his cigar.

"Have a beer," he said. "Or something else. It's a beautiful day and we're in a beautiful town and your wife tells me I should read your novel. She says it would interest me. Not many do these days, but I'll follow her advice. You've had quite a success with it, haven't you?"

Sheila and Ronnie

"Choked to death on her own spite, I should say."

Tony let his cousin's letter slip from his hand and lit a cigarette. Fifty years ago the girls had been best friends, and not only because Sheila had a pony which she was happy to share with his cousin whose parents couldn't afford one. Now Lizzie wrote, "She had of course become enormously fat, I expect really that was what killed her..."

Fifty years ago... When Tony spent Easter and summer holidays mostly at the big Victorian manse in Kenraith, he would position himself around twelve o'clock every morning at the bow window of the first-floor rarely used drawing-room in the hope of seeing Sheila go down the street to do her mother's shopping. A little basket dangled from her arm, like an illustration in a Ladybird book. In those days seventeen-year-old girls still dressed like their mothers and Sheila would be wearing a skirt that came to knee level and was stretched tight over her bottom. Her hips swayed and the bottom wiggled and it was the sexiest thing Tony had ever yet seen, in real life rather than in the cinema or the photographs he pinned over his bed at school, sexier even than the legs of a pantomime Principal Boy. On days when it was raining or her mother required no shopping, he felt cheated. Nobody mentioned his daily vigil and he often wondered if anyone was aware of it.

He pressed the button of his espresso machine and took his coffee out on to the terrace. The morning shimmer of the day's heat-haze trembled over the town five kilometres away and he didn't know how many metres below his little house. Dampness glittered on the leaves of the plum-trees in the orchard beyond the terrace. He thought of telephoning Lizzie in distant Edinburgh. Later perhaps, in the evening, when a few glasses of white wine might have loosened what remained of her Presbyterian tongue... There weren't many people he cared to talk to now. Lizzie was one of the few, precisely because she belonged so completely to the years that were lost. But not often, not often.

Conversation with Sheila had never got far. When she came, evenings or wet afternoons, to see Lizzie at the manse, they played cards or Monopoly. She was good and acquisitive at Monopoly and always built houses and hotels on the most profitable sites.

"Easy to see she's her father's daughter," Aunt Cathie said.

The father, Jimmy Yorston, had started as a scrap-dealer, now, besides his big breaker's yard – "that eyesore" – owned half a dozen petrol-stations and car dealerships. He didn't attend church, though his wife did and brought Sheila with her. On cold Sundays Sheila wore a soft camel coat with a pink chiffon scarf. Older women remarked on her high heels. "He drinks," they said of Jimmy Yorston, "half a bottle a day, I'm told."

"At least."

There was a hawk hovering over the plum-trees. Tony stretched out on an old-fashioned deck chair with wooden struts. His black cat, Stendhal, jumped on to his lap. He stroked the plushy fur, scratched him behind the ears and was rewarded with a contented purr.

There had been dances. Sheila wore long dresses – gowns? – in material which rustled. There was competition to dance with her. Tony sometimes managed to get her for a waltz. When he pressed himself against her, he found her brassiere as hard and unyielding as a cricketer's box. For a moment she wouldn't resist, then drew back, as if her mother might be watching. He contrived once to kiss her in a dark passage. Her lips were soft and damp. "Oh," she said, "oh. We mustn't. Someone might see. That's enough."

The hawk still hovered. The cat continued to purr. Tony sighed. So long ago.

He had been reading the other day an essay or article about life in a big accountancy firm. There was a girl called Katie, the young assistant to the head of the Far East Retail Division, or something like that. She wore knee-length grey woollen shorts. The author remarked that these shorts provoked "insistent and inappropriate thoughts", which threatened "to subvert the firm's entire rationale" because they invited an awkward desire to engage in sex rather than work... If Sheila had worn knee-length grey woollen shorts, would he have been able to obey her command, "that's enough"?

They all, until they were in the Upper Sixth, wore shorts at his healthy high-minded school in the Yorkshire Dales. These aroused few erotic thoughts in Tony. Not so Graham, with whom he shared a study; he salivated over the tight navy shorts of a fourth-former called Douglas. "I'd do anything to take the cane to him," he said. "Stuff it, you're showing off," Tony said. "Stuff him I would," Graham said.

When Tony showed him a photograph of Sheila he had snitched from Lizzie, Graham said, "Some heifer, if you like heifers."

Tony's parents were missionaries in India. He seldom saw them, or indeed thought of them, and found it difficult to write the obligatory Sunday-after-chapel letter. Even in those days, boys whose father was in the Foreign Office or worked for an oil company would be flown out for the summer holidays, but the Mission Society which employed his parents couldn't afford such extravagance. That was why Tony spent most holidays at the manse. It was his grandfather, disapproving of the man his daughter had married, who paid the fees for Tony's Spartan school. He would take Tony for a week's fishing on the Aberdeenshire Dee in April and a week's skiing in

Zermatt in January, and warn him off religion. The warning had not been very necessary.

His aunt and uncle didn't really approve of Lizzie's friendship with Sheila. "A proper little madam", Aunt Cathie called her, adding, in an unusually unguarded moment, "you'd never think to see her strut down the street that Jimmy Yorston's grandfather was a tink." By "tink" she meant gypsy. Tony liked the idea, rolled it round in his imagination; it promised something unbridled which Sheila kept concealed. "There's bad blood there," Aunt Cathie said, "and Jimmy Yorston drinks like a fish. But you'll forget I said that, Tony." It was a relief to her when Sheila went off to boarding-school. She hoped it would break the friendship, and indeed it did begin to fray as Lizzie acquired wider interests, even before she became political, this also however to her mother's distress.

Sheila being away at school emboldened Tony to write to her. She replied. The correspondence became regular. The sight of her blue envelopes with his name and address in her wide-looped handwriting excited him, though he found the matter of her letters distressingly thin and banal. They were full of sighs and complaints. She hated the uniform she had to wear; "horrible shapeless baggy skirts." But when her third letter closed with a row of kisses, he pressed it to his lips and slept with it under his pillow, as in his icy room he nightly undressed her. He ended his reply with the words, "love or what you will" and added kisses of his own. But when they met on their next holidays, they still found nothing to say, and, though she permitted him to hug and kiss her, she brushed his exploratory and nervous hand away from her thighs or breasts.

The telephone rang. He dislodged Stendhal with apologies and went to answer it. His son, child of his last marriage.

"Antoine," he said, "nothing up, is there?"

"No, I'm just calling to say we won't get to you before this evening. About seven. That OK?."

"Sure. The dinner will not demand precise timing."

"Good. Look forward..."

"Me too. Oh, and Antoine, remind me, what's the new girl called?"

"Sonia. I already told you."

"I know you did, but my memory, you know. Sonia. I'll write it down. See you. "

"See you, Dad."

"Drive carefully," he said, but the connection was already broken.

He adored Antoine, hoped she was a nice girl. Some of them hadn't been.

The hawk had gone and the sky was empty. He gave himself a whisky-and-soda, a very weak one.

Really there was nothing, or very little, wrong with his memory. It was an act he put on, for Antoine, but also for others. Nevertheless he made a note of the girl's name. It was like crossing his fingers.

On the last day of the summer holidays of – it must have been – 1955, he went round to the Yorstons' house to say goodbye to Sheila. It was a new house of glaring red brick. His aunt condemned it as "showy". He hadn't visited before, hadn't in truth dared to, suspecting – rightly, he supposed now – that Jimmy Yorston disapproved of him, thought him stuck-up. But it was afternoon and he should be at work. He rang the bell. No answer, except the barking of her mother's West Highland terriers. Perhaps she was in the garden? But he found only her young brother, Ronnie, playing cricket by himself against a brick wall.

"I was looking for Sheila. Is she about?"

"She's gone to town with Mum. Shopping. Clothes-shopping. They wanted me to go, but I said "no thanks".

The boy went to the local school and spoke with the accent that Sheila had now lost, more or less. He was a thin dark-skinned boy with curly black hair. "He's a throwback. You can see the gypsy in him," Aunt Cathie said.

"Do you play cricket?"

"Yes."

"Would you bowl to me? There's a net Dad put up at the bottom of the garden."

"OK, why not?"

Perhaps Sheila would return and be pleased to find him entertaining her little brother? But she didn't, and that autumn their correspondence became less frequent and then died away. Lizzie told him she was no longer best friends with Sheila, no longer friends at all.

"I realised we have nothing in common." Lizzie was becoming serious.

"She thinks of nothing but clothes," she said.

He went up to Oxford and into a new life. He found himself a girlfriend, a blonde from Stuttgart called Magda. She had none of Sheila's inhibitions and went to bed with him happily in the afternoons. At Easter she invited him to Germany. Her parents were welcoming, her father speaking without embarrassment about his experiences in the Wehrmacht and his time as a POW in England. He had been in a camp just outside Oxford." A beautiful city, which is why I was so happy that Magda should study English there. It is time the past was forgotten. There was much evil and much stupidity. " Wolfgang adored his daughter, but, to Tony's surprise, didn't seem to care that she had sex with him. It didn't last, but he would always be grateful to her. At Oxford he took up acting. In his last year they brought their production of *Twelfth Night* to the Edinburgh Fringe. Tony played the Duke, Orsino, and fell in love with the girl who played Viola. That wouldn't last either. He loved the theatre, but realised that he lacked the talent to make a career as an actor. So he applied for and got a job with the BBC. In a couple of years he was producing radio plays. Lizzie told him that Sheila was getting married.

"To George Innes. He's fat and red-faced and ten years older than she is. I don't suppose you ever met him or would remember him if you did. He's in construction, as they say. That means he puts up horrible houses all over the place."

"Well off then?"

"Well off. You wouldn't catch Sheila marrying a poor man. He'll keep her in clothes. Jewels too, probably. They say he can't keep his eyes off her. Well, you used to be like that, remember?"

"Was I?"

"You know you were."

Lizzie was spending the night in his flat in Pembridge Gardens; she had just completed the Aldermaston march.

"You had a lucky escape," she said.

"Oh, I don't think I was ever in danger of being caught."

All the same he still dreamed of Sheila sometimes and they were good dreams.

"They say Jimmy Yorston's drinking himself to death. He's had one go of DTs already, according to Mum."

"She never liked him, did she?"

"Can't stand him. Disapproves strongly. She may be right."

"There was a brother, wasn't there?" he said. "What was his name?"

"Ronnie. Very thick."

"So what's happened to him?"

"Oh, he works with Jimmy. Will take over the scrap business. He never went away to school, remember. Jimmy didn't want him to get grand ideas at a fancy school. Or so he said. Grand ideas indeed – he gave him a sportscar for his eighteenth birthday and now I'm told he has got himself a Jaguar E-type."

"You wouldn't know an E-type if you saw one, Liz."

"No, I wouldn't and I've no wish to."

But Tony remembered him as an eager twelve-year-old who talked cricket happily when his tongue was at last unlocked.

He finished his whisky-and-soda, picked up his blackthorn stick and toddled off – the way he thought of his walk now – up the hill to the village to have lunch at the Rendez-vous des Bergers. He had never seen a shepherd there but the lamb cutlets were perfectly cooked. Because of Antoine's visit he restricted himself to a half-litre of the local pink wine. He ate outside so that he could smoke while waiting for food and between courses. There was an English party at the next table, but he didn't speak to them. He lit a cigar with his coffee, paid his bill and returned home for an hour's kip. An easy life. He'd earned it. Stendhal joined him on the bed, approving of sleep, like all cats.

He had another memory of Ronnie, one he had never shared with Liz. Or indeed anyone, not that there was anyone else who would know who Ronnie was.

It was in the middle Sixties, melancholy autumn.

One night he had dinner with Graham in Soho – Chez Victor in Wardour Street when it was still a French restaurant. They were both in limbo. Graham's wife had started divorce proceedings and Tony's first wife, Linda, had walked out the week before. So they drank deep and told each other they were happy.

"I felt free when she told me she no longer loved me."

Which of them had said that? Both perhaps.

"It was a mistake from the start."

That was certainly Graham.

"An experiment," he said, "that's gone wrong. Do you remember Douglas?"

"The navy shorts?"

"Exactly. I might go on to a club I know. Fancy coming?"

"Why not? But some brandy first, don't you think."

"Several brandies first."

The club was in an alley off... he couldn't recall which street – Lexington perhaps? That end of Soho anyway. It was the usual sort of place: a grubby nameplate, a spy-hole and a bottle-nosed doorman who greeted Graham as Andy and shoved a book at him to sign Tony in.

"Whatever name you please," he said. "It's the law, don't mean nothing."

They mounted a rickety wooden stair. The club was on the first floor. An unexpectedly spacious room with Parisian posters tacked to the walls – Le Chat Noir and Mistinguette – that sort of thing. A blond boy was playing jazz on the piano, rather badly. He raised a hand to Graham. Three or four couples were dancing in perfunctory fashion.

Graham said, "We'd better put ginger ale in the brandy here. That's what I recommend."

"Come here often, do you?" Tony said.

"Home from home. Better than home. It's not often raided," he said.

He was a little drunk. Well, they both were.

A boy dressed as a sailor approached.

"Want to dance, Andy?"

Graham waved him away.

"Merchant navy," he said. "Merchandise. It's the piano-player I come for."

In a little the blond boy stopped playing, closed the piano lid, pushed the stool in, came over and kissed Graham on the cheek.

"Long time, Andy," he said.

"Too long for me." He got to his feet, holding on to the boy's arm. "You'll be all right on your own, Tony? Things to discuss."

Tony lifted his glass, "I'll be fine."

"Don't have anything to do with Johnny."

"Johnny?"

"The sailor-boy. The merchandise. He gave me crabs once."

"Thanks for the warning. Not necessary though."

He drank his brandy-and-ginger, ordered another. The place amused him, he told himself, as an observer. Only that. It was sad, yes, but where isn't? He may have fallen asleep.

There was a hand on his shoulder and a voice saying, "You taught me how to bowl leg-breaks."

A slightly built young man with dark curly hair. He was wearing a charcoal-grey city suit, cream shirt and maroon tie. The hand which he now removed from Tony's shoulder was larger than his general appearance suggested.

"I nearly went away when I saw you. But then I thought: I'm here, he's here, so what's to run away from? Do you remember me? Ronnie Yorston."

"Of course, but..." or something like that.

"Surprised, eh?"

"Have some brandy. Is this where we say, do you come here often?"

"When I'm in London on business, yes, usually. It relaxes me, and do I need relaxation tonight! I've been putting through a deal with an Eastern European country, Bulgaria it was."

"What sort of deal?"

"Scrap. That's what I'm in, still, the family business, remember?"

They talked for a bit, drank some more brandy, then Ronnie said, "I was hoping to meet someone. He's not here. Maybe we should go."

In the street, looking for a taxi, Tony said, "Where now?"

"This is where one of us says, your place or mine."

"All right. Your place or mine?"

"Mine's the Savoy. That's where I always stay in London."

"Mine then."

Back in the flat – Hertford Street, they'd moved up-market from Notting Hill – Tony opened a bottle of Remy Martin.

"No need for ginger ale with this," he said.

"Are you married?"

"Was. No longer, it seems. Why?"

"Woman's hand. In the furnishings. Cheers."

Tony put an LP on the gramophone. Charlie Parker playing Cole Porter. "My heart belongs to Daddy."

"I used to watch you," Ronnie said. "Bet you didn't know that."

"I used to watch your sister."

Ronnie came and sat on the arm of Tony's chair.

"What about it?" he said. "Do you like me as much as you liked her?"

"Why not?"

Later Ronnie said, "Did you ever fuck my sister?"

"Never gave me the chance."

He ran his finger along the line of Ronnie's lips.

"You have very beautiful brown eyes."

"My gypsy blood. Hers are piggy."

They hadn't seemed so to Tony.

"Now she's getting fat," Ronnie said, "they're really piggy."

In the morning, cooking bacon and eggs, Tony said, "Didn't get value of your expensive room in the Savoy, did you?"

"Company pays. I only do this sort of thing in London, you know.

After breakfast Ronnie asked if he might take a shower. He emerged with a towel wrapped round him and his dark skin gleaming.

"Do this again, can we?"

"Why not?"

Ronnie went to dress, returned looking the smart young businessman.

"When I used to watch you," he said, "I wanted this though I didn't know it then. I'll give you a bell when I'm next down."

He did so twice. The first time Tony had a date with the girl who became his second wife a couple of years later. The second, well, that was a bit of a disaster. Ronnie arrived drunk, stinking drunk, with a Spanish boy. Tony couldn't wait to be rid of them. And that was that.

Stendhal came and lay on his chest digging his claws gently into Tony's neck.

"I felt guilty," he said, "no reason why I should but I did, as if I'd let him down. You wouldn't understand that, would you? Cats have no sense of guilt, have they? Feline wisdom, you'd say. You're probably right."

He eased himself out of bed, put on his trousers, and espadrilles on his feet.

"Time to prepare supper for Master Antoine. You'll be pleased to see him, won't you, Stendhal. He's bringing a new girl. Be nice to her, whatever. On your best behaviour, cat."

He began to prepare a casserole of red cabbage, apples and onions; he would add Toulouse sausages later. It was one of Antoine's favourites, always had been, and no trouble. He would roast potatoes in goose fat to go with it. He hoped the girl Sonia was a hearty eater. There was an apricot tart from the patisserie to follow, and Roquefort cheese.

The last time he had seen Sheila was at Aunt Cathie's funeral. Seven years ago? Nearer ten, now he thought of it. Didn't matter. She had certainly put on weight, though how much he didn't realise till she came to the funeral tea at the hotel and took off her mink coat. You wouldn't call her sexy now, though she behaved as if she still was. And – yes – now he looked closely – her eyes were piggy, as Ronnie had said. Yet somewhere in the mountain of flesh lurked the girl he had so intensely wanted. There wasn't much to talk about, but then there never had been. He asked her about Ronnie.

"Oh, we don't speak. He lives in Spain now..."

"You had a lucky escape, didn't you," Lizzie said when all the guests – some of whom you couldn't really describe as mourners – had gone.

"What happened to the brother? She seemed a bit evasive about him."

"Well, he was no good. A failure. I blame Jimmy Yorston, who spoiled him, you know. Anyway he ran through the money, took so much out of the business it was on the verge of bankruptcy... George and Sheila bought him out. Didn't pay much if I know them. It's doing very well again now."

"Sad story".

"I suppose so. You never knew him though, did you?"

"Not really. I remember playing cricket with him in their garden. His father had put up a net. He seemed like a nice kid."

"Oh, always pleasant enough. But thick and a fool with money. I don't know what he does in Spain. Nothing much, I suppose. It's cheap there, isn't it."

"Yes, it's cheap. It's still cheap, I think, though not as cheap as it was in Franco's day."

"People used to sponge on him, they say. Hangers-on. They had a lot of the money."

"Sad story," he said again.

"There are sadder," Lizzie said. "People who've never had anything, never had the chances he threw away. I don't find it easy to feel sorry for people like Ronnie Yorston."

"No, I suppose not."

Tony's grandfather died, very old, left him enough to enable him to retire from the BBC before he was pushed out, buy this house in the Dordogne. Antoine's mother left him. He wrote a couple of crime novels and made notes for a book on Stendhal – the author, not the cat. He got by. Sometimes he thought that was as much as you could hope for.

He put the casserole in the oven and went out on to the terrace again. The light was golden and restful, and usually he loved it. But today, this late afternoon turning to evening, he didn't know, he couldn't settle, and there was nothing he could bring himself to read. He let a cigar and called Lizzie on his mobile…

"It's me. Thanks for your letter. About Sheila."

"No big news but I thought you'd want to know."

"It's brought back the past."

"Well, you'll enjoy that, won't you, now that you've contracted out as they say. Do you know, we became quite friends again in these last years, since George died. I suppose she was lonely."

"You said it was spite killed her."

"Did I? If you say so, and yes, she was spiteful, but I quite enjoyed her company, even though she was always trying to make use of me."

"Don't suppose you stood for that, Liz."

"Not much. She stayed with me here a few times. I was amazed when she first asked if she could. Then, saving on hotel bills, I thought. But I quite enjoyed having her and talking about old times. There's not many I can do that with. But, you know, she was extraordinary. A couple of years back, she rang up after she'd been visiting, not a word of thanks but she chatted happily for half an hour. Then, not two minutes after I had put the phone down, it rang again and there she was. 'I forgot,' she said, 'Ronnie Yorston's dead.' That's what she called him – Ronnie Yorston – her own brother. Don't you think that was strange?"

"You said they didn't get on."

"Not at all. All the same..."

A car turned off the public road coming towards his house.

"Must ring off," he said, "that's Antoine arriving with a girl. A new girl."

"Give him my love. They don't last, do they? His girls, I mean."

"This one may. You never know."

"Come and see me sometime. There's not many of us left."

"No," he said, "there's not. Why don't you come here?"

"Perhaps, I just might..."

He switched off and went out to greet his son. They embraced.

"This is Sonia, Dad."

"Well, I suppose it is."

She was a very pretty girl, lovely really. She wore knee-length blue lycra shorts. Anyone's eyes would turn to watch her go down the street.

Venetian Whispers

I don't know if this story is true. I had it myself at third, or even fourth, hand. So, in the Chinese whispers of anecdotage, some distortion of fact is likely. Nevertheless, as they say in Italy – and it is an Italian or rather Venetian tale – *se non è vero, è ben trovato.*

Some years back, I wrote a book about Byron (now out of print, if you want to know). As a result I was invited to speak to the Byron Society. This was not a success; my fault, I had lunched too well with Auberon Waugh and continued drinking through the afternoon. A few days later I got a letter from a retired diplomat who had attended my lecture, and had a story that might interest me. Would I come and have lunch with him? At the Ritz, he added, as if I might be in need of such inducement. Despite the embarrassment which the memory of my Byron evening caused me, I accepted.

We talked a little, mostly about nothing much. Then he took a sheet of yellowed paper from a folder he had rested against the table-leg.

"What do you make of that?"

And, as I looked at the sketch, blurred, shadowed, yet made with strong, assured lines, he recited:

"The Moon is up, and yet it is not Night –
"Sunset divides the sky with her – a sea
"Of glory streams along the Alpine height
"Of blue Friuli's mountains...

"Catches the mood, doesn't it?" he said. "It's Turner, you know. At least I'm pretty sure it's Turner."

"I wouldn't know," I said. "It's good, I can see that. But I'm ignorant, no expert. Did Turner ever illustrate *Childe Harold*? I hadn't heard that he did."

Again I felt embarrassed. It seemed as if my professed knowledge of Byron was to be proved inadequate.

"No record that he did," he said. "But look at that line, look at these clouds, I'd take my oath... Rum business, art – you'll know that Turner said that... and my story's rum enough. It's not really mine, but my great-uncle's..."

He paused and sipped his wine.

"I've led a very respectable life," he said. "Finished as an ambassador. Not a very distinguished embassy, I admit. My Uncle Eddie was not so respectable. He lived most of his adult life in Italy. People with his tastes did, often, in his day, you understand. He was a poet of sorts, a dilettante who spent half his life making notes for a Byron book that never got written. In the late Thirties he used to go to Venice for the winter. He loved it then, and it was the Italian city least enthusiastic about Fascism. This is his story, which he told me shortly before his death, just after the war. I was at Cambridge then, Trinity – you were at Trinity too, I think? Like Byron and Uncle Eddie himself.

"He'd got through most of his money by then. So the days of grand hotels such as the Hôtel des Bains where Thomas Mann installed Aschenbach were over. He used to stay in a little *pensione* in a *calle* fifty yards off the Grand Canal. Over the years he had become friendly with the proprietor, partly because – though Ettore was a married man with a family – Uncle Eddie was not long in discerning that he shared his tastes. Common enough, of course, in Venice as elsewhere – didn't Châteaubriand call it 'an unnatural city?'

"Forgive me if my story seems slow. But I like to set the scene. And if you are to judge its credibility... Anyway, it was the late autumn turning to winter of 1939. Italy, as you know, was not yet at war, but ever since the Abyssinian affair, feeling against England and the English was running high. Back in Florence Uncle

Eddie had been made to feel *persona non grata.* There had been a bit of what he called 'fuss'. Ettore commiserated; he found Uncle Eddie *simpatico.* They would sit drinking white wine or grappa and listening to the rain as darkness closed in.

"'Ah... Venice, lost and won, / Her thirteen hundred years of freedom done, / Sinks, like a sea-weed, unto whence she rose...' sighed my uncle in his distress.

"'The milord,' Ettore pressed my uncle's hand, 'the Lord Byron,' and then, shyly at first, told this story.

"'Why only then?' I asked my uncle. 'Perhaps,' he said, 'because we both sensed that all things were drifting to an end. I don't know. I was only so touched that he now chose to share this confidence...'

"Ettore was, he said, a descendant, great-grandson would it be? – of Byron's mistress Margarita Cogni. You remember – indeed I think you quote in your book – that Byron delighted in this woman 'with the strength of an Amazon and the temper of Medea' and liked the fact that she was illiterate and so 'could not plague me with letters.' Ettore, my uncle said, was very different – the mildest mannered of men and well read in Venetian, Italian and even English literature. But he was proud of his connection, though modestly stopped short of saying that he was descended from Byron himself. Byron called Venice 'the mask of Italy'. I've never been quite sure what he meant...

"According to Ettore, this English painter arrived with a commission from he didn't know whom. Byron was happy to lodge him in the Palazzo Mocenigo. I suppose one guest more or less in that tumbling household made no difference. But Margarita took against him. He wasn't a *galant'uomo*, she said, but a grumpy, surly fellow who seemed to place himself, as an artist, on a leve! with the milord. This offended her. He didn't know, she said, how to behave. He was dirty in mind and body – *sporchissimo*

– a wonderful word to spit out, with z's rather than s's really, I suppose, in Venetian. But Byron took pleasure in his company. I imagine that Turner's naturalness – I'm assuming it was Turner – and the seriousness with which he took his work while being entirely free of pretentiousness appealed to Byron, who choked off Tom Moore's rhapsodies with his 'Damme, Tom, don't be poetical.'

"Who had given Turner his commission? John Murray? His patron Lord Egremont? Uncle Eddie didn't know and it doesn't matter. But it's clear what it was: to illustrate a new edition of *Childe Harold*, and he had come to Venice to discuss with Byron which scenes in that vast travelogue would make the most dramatic and Romantic pictures. Of course, being in Venice, he found things to draw every day. Margarita, incidentally, thought nothing of his work. I suppose her taste inclined to the geometric accuracy of Guardi and Canaletto. But she may have disliked the work because she disliked the man. You must find that yourself as a reviewer...

"Byron, Ettore insisted, didn't share Margarita's distaste. The painter amused him. He might be – this was Uncle Eddie's interpretation – a cockney, but he wasn't cockneyfied like Leigh Hunt, or indeed poor 'piss-a-bed' Keats. All the same, Turner may have felt more at ease with Fletcher, Byron's valet. They went out on the town together. Fletcher had always had a taste for whores – you remember how angry Byron was when Fletcher introduced young Robert Rushton, his boy servant, to that sort of company. I like to think that Fletcher presented Turner, never without a propensity for low-life, with that eminently useful *Tariffa delle putane di Venezia*. But it seems not to have been enough to satisfy him..."

"What do you mean by that?" I asked.

"Just the question I put to Uncle Eddie. He said, 'A painter lives through his eye and by his hand.'"

"Enigmatic."

"Perhaps..." My host paused. "Think we should have some brandy, Armagnac perhaps? Do you know Evelyn Waugh's joke about the Turkish ambassador and Lolita?"

"Yes," I offered, "'In my country we do not like to read about such things; we prefer to see them.'"

"Exactly. That, it seems, was Turner's opinion too. He was a voyeur, Ettore said. The painter's eye, I suppose. So it wasn't enough to go on the town with Fletcher and bring his whores back to the palazzo. His curiosity was insatiable and soon, it seems he was spying on Byron. Fletcher, according to Ettore, caught him at it and boxed his ears. Then, his suspicions aroused, he found occasion to examine the painter's sketchbook. Most of the drawings were innocent enough – the sort of thing I showed you. There were also some pornographic sketches, which I dare say Fletcher in another mood would have appreciated. They were beautifully done, erotic certainly but imbued with distaste. However, what really put the cat among the Venetian pigeons and threw Fletcher into a panic was that a couple of them showed Byron on the job. In one he was coupling with Margarita, legs entwined, and it was so lifelike, Uncle Eddie said, that you could all but smell the sweat and semen. The other was even more alarming. The poet was lying naked on a couch with a curly-headed boy astride him. The boy had turned his head towards the hidden artist and was laughing, as if with an accomplice. 'Lubricious – terribly exciting,' was Uncle Eddie's verdict."

"Your Uncle actually saw these drawings?"

"Oh yes. They'd been kept in Ettore's family. I like to think the boy was one of those Shelley described as 'wretches that seem to have lost the gait and physiognomy of men'. Awful prig, Shelley, like so many high-minded revolutionaries."

He took a cigar from a leather case.

"As to the precise course of events, Uncle Eddie was vague, Ettore too, one assumes. Fletcher was certainly in a stew. After all, if the painter had had access to Byron's antechamber and been able to peer through the keyhole or from behind a curtain, then Fletcher as the valet was likely to be blamed. Somehow he ejected Turner – if it was Turner..." he looked at the drawing again. "Oh yes, it must have been Turner, don't you think? And he confiscated the sketchbook."

"Why not destroy it? And how did they come to be in Ettore's possession?"

"My guess is that Margarita suspected something – perhaps Fletcher dropped a hint in his cups; they may have been in the habit of drinking together. Ettore believed that when Byron abandoned her and took up with the Countess Guiccioli, Fletcher stepped into the breach as it were. 'Moreover,' Ettore told Uncle Eddie, 'the boy has a look of me when I was young and was being chased by all the foreign pederasts in Venice. I think he may have been Margarita's younger brother.'

"But that's beside the point. Somehow she prevailed on Fletcher to hand them over. Perhaps she hoped to use them as material for blackmail. On the other hand, Ettore said, there was a belief in the family that Turner himself became her lover on his later visit to Venice, after Byron's death, and it may even be that he gave the sketches to her as – what? – a souvenir of both himself and her dear milord. Which would mean the story of the row with Fletcher was apocryphal."

"And the other drawings?" I asked. "May I see them? Why have you kept them concealed? They must be worth the Lord knows what."

"That was Ettore's idea. He wanted to provide for his old age, you see. So he gave this single one to my uncle, that he might have it authenticated. But it was winter 1939, remember? Uncle Eddie was reluctant to leave

Italy, but he got out at the last minute, in a hurry. When at last he got back to Venice in 1946, Ettore and his wife were both dead, and his son, who was a Communist, knew nothing of any drawings. He'd fought with the Partisans and for that reason either the Fascists or the Germans had ransacked the *pensione*. There was nothing, he told Uncle Eddie, nothing, it had been an 'extermination'. He may have been speaking the truth, or he may have simply disliked or been suspicious of Eddie. He was, as I say, a Communist and therefore a stern moralist. Be that as it may, after more than a hundred years the drawings had vanished, evaporated. Sad, don't you think?"

"Sad indeed. And this one? Has it been authenticated?"

"The experts won't commit themselves. As for the dealers, they say 'Yes maybe' if they think I want to sell it and 'maybe not' when it's clear I don't. To be honest, I don't much care. Besides, who can tell? It's agreeable to think that, somewhere, there may yet survive Turner drawings of Byron rogering Margarita Cogni and being ridden by a curly-headed Venetian boy. Rum story, eh?"

Rum indeed. I wondered, and still wonder, what truth there was in it. Perhaps one day some dingy antique shop in a noisome *calle* will yield the answer. Or perhaps not.

Bertram's Funeral

They knew him in the village as "the writer", but none of them had read his books. That didn't make them remarkable. His success, once considerable, was a bit back. When he brought out a novel now, it was reviewed as one in a batch, often at the tail end, and his telephone didn't ring. He read interviews with more fashionable novelists instead.

The cottage garden was overgrown and the wind bent the brown thistle-heads. It was too early for a gin. Most days that wouldn't have bothered or stopped him, but he was going to the funeral of an old friend. He didn't want to topple into the grave.

The old friend was a painter. When Graham started out as a writer, he had known people who went and did all sorts of different things. His own father had been an engineer and the people he put in his first two books were engaged in the sort of occupations that demand regular hours; he had characters who wouldn't themselves read novels. Now he knew only other writers, painters, failed actresses, and the layabouts drawing dole money who were numerous in the county where he had come to live. That was after his wife left him, or he left her. He couldn't be sure which had made the decisive move, if indeed there had been one – the marriage came to the point when there were no leaves left on the tree.

The cat came to the window. He let it in and it asked for food. He scratched it behind the ear, but it shook its head, and he went to the refrigerator and took a chunk of cod he had cooked yesterday and put some on a saucer. He gave himself that gin to keep the cat company.

It was a beautiful cat, a long-haired Red Self, half Persian. He had swithered about having him neutered, and then done nothing, and put up with the spraying.

The cat was called Trajan, after the emperor, and slept on Graham's bed and sometimes nibbled his ear in the dark.

The church was five miles away. He drove through the lanes at twenty-five miles an hour, hooting at junctions. He sat upright in his big black car. The wings were spattered with mud. He had had the car twenty years, and the marque was long discontinued as a result of a series of mergers and what they called rationalisations. It would last some time yet. He didn't do 3,000 miles in a year and usually he remembered to garage it in the old barn which went with the cottage. He sang, off-key, as he drove:

We plough the fields and scatter
The good seed on the land,
But it is fed and watered
By God's almighty hand...

He didn't go to church now, except for funerals, but he sang hymns while driving, shaving, or taking a bath.

There were already a lot of people in the church, and, in the English fashion, they had filled it from the back, so that he had to advance well up the aisle to find a place. He dropped on his knees on a worn hassock, extruding stuffing, to say a long-remembered, long-disused prayer. "Visit this habitation, we beseech thee, oh Lord..." Why did the word, "beseech", vanished from ordinary parlance, where, in any case, if used, it would be condemned as feeble, sound so right here?

He sat back and fingered his black tie. The last funeral he had attended, he had been the only man wearing a black tie, and he had hesitated before knotting it this morning. He had looked at himself in the glass, with the tie dangling loose, at the face he had not liked when young, though some found it attractive, but which he had grown fond of as it deteriorated, and then he had sighed, and knotted the tie, thinking, as he seldom did, of his mother who used to ask if he had put on clean underclothes in case he was knocked down by a car and taken to hospital.

There was a good turnout for Bertram. Graham had been to services at crematoria where there had been so few that a hymn was out of the question. He made a point of going to the funerals of friends, and there were a lot of them now as gin, whisky, cigarettes, anxiety, loss of hope, took their toll. He hated crematoria though. The assumption there was that the dead were simply inconveniences to be shuffled off; his presence was a silent protest.

A woman, heavily veiled, was advancing up the aisle. That was perhaps a bit much. One of Bertram's old mistresses making a point, staking a claim, stealing the scene? Then she passed him and he saw it was a young black man with dreadlocks. The trailing skirt he had caught in the corner of his eye belonged to an overcoat. The young man's head was bowed, which was why it had looked as if he was wearing a veil. Graham felt a giggle steal up on him: it was a joke Bertram would have liked.

Besides the mistresses, Bertram had had three wives, not concurrently, and six or seven children. There might have been other children born out of wedlock, Graham didn't know. He had scattered his image freely enough. Graham made a sign to Annie, the second wife, the one he had known best and liked least.

The vicar read the Twenty-third Psalm, from green pastures to the valley of the shadow of death. Tears came into Graham's eyes. Another lesson: in my Father's house are many mansions... as many, he wondered, as the bed-sitters of Pimlico, where he had been living in a drab room with yellow walls, when he had first met Bertram? He had shared it with a young man called Richard.

Neither of them had any work, but they spoke of how they would dominate the world. One evening, Richard said: "Do you and Bertram have to be drunk every night?"

They stood to sing. "The ancient Prince of hell/Hath risen with purpose fell..." "Ein feste Burg ist unser Gott..." In his youth Graham worked at night, often finishing at two, three in the morning. Then he went out into the city and walked. It was a time when even the bad things that happened seemed fruitful.

"The blessing of God Almighty, Father, Son and Holy Ghost..." Eight young men, at least three of them Bertram's sons, carried the coffin out of the church.

The rain had stopped. Bertram had loved painting rain. He did it well, better than anything else. There was one painting he had kept for years, refusing to sell, of ploughed fields in rain. The fields rose from the bottom of the canvas towards a line of winter trees. It was grey and brown, half a dozen different greys and browns, except for a dot of pink placed by a church spire that rose between the trees. There was a figure in the foreground, but Graham couldn't remember if it had been male or female. It didn't matter. It was just there, and maybe it was meant to be insignificant. Then Bertram sold the painting and probably it was hung in an American gallery now.

He squashed his hat on to his head and buttoned his overcoat. It was an eastern county and all winds were sharp from October to March. There was a big sky and the chug of a tractor. Jackdaws flew about the little church with its square tower. He was standing near a woman whom he recognised as his daughter. He hadn't seen her for six or seven years, and the line of her j aw was stronger than it used to be. She hadn't seen him, her gaze was fixed on the grave. Old words floated towards him. He took off his hat and shoved it into his pocket. He bent his head. Bertram was her godfather. That was why she was here, and it was right. They would have to speak, later. He used to call her "Nutkin". He doubted if she would like to be called "Nutkin" now. Her coat was good and expensive. She had her arm round a young blond boy. It must be his grandson.

One of the young men holding one of the cords let go too soon. The coffin lurched feet first into the hole. For a moment it looked as if Bertram would have to be buried vertical. Then adjustments were made. The descent was accomplished. Handfuls of earth were thrown. The crowd began to disperse. Graham waited, then scratched up some of the blue-grey clay soil, and let it fall on his friend. That was that. He wondered if they had put a paintbrush and palette in the coffin. He hoped they had, not that he would ask for a typewriter in his. There wouldn't be this sort of turnout when it came to his turn to turn in.

He touched his daughter on the shoulder.

"Susie," he said, not daring "Nutkin".

His fingers left smears of clay on the good navy-blue cloth. He hoped she wouldn't notice till she got home and that she wouldn't then connect it with him.

"You should have let me know you were coming. I'd have given you lunch."

The boy was looking at him. He had the kind of face illustrators used to draw in school stories, for the hero – frank, open, manly; obsolete, unusable epithets. Graham thought of other boys he knew, or saw around on his rare visits to London, and wondered how long this boy could keep that look in today's world.

Susie said nothing. She left the word "lunch" hanging in the thin autumn air.

"You don't know me," he said to the boy. "I'm your grandfather."

How old was he? Thirteen, fourteen? Something like that. He was a nice-looking boy, and he had nice manners, because he smiled now, not embarrassed, even as if pleased to meet him.

"This is the first funeral I've ever been to," he said. "I've only come because I'm on half-term."

"Good," Graham said. "I'm glad you've come, Susie. Old Bertram was always fond of you."

"He sent me a painting last Christmas," she said. "I could see it was good, but I only hang abstracts. But he said it was valuable and I suppose it is."

"Take it to his dealer if you want it valued. But I should hang on to it. Bertram said his paintings will be worth more in ten, fifteen years than they are now. That was quite recently. He always had a good eye for market values."

He hoped he didn't sound bitter. The words could seem bitter, but they weren't meant that way. Still, they helped get over the awkwardness and ease them on their way from the churchyard to the house. But the awkwardness couldn't be altogether avoided.

"Is your mother here? I didn't see her in the church."

It was mad that he hadn't thought they might be here. "No," she said. "She's not. In fact, she's ill. In fact she's in hospital."

The wind twitched at the thin branches, ruffled his hair. He pushed his hat back on his head.

"I'm sorry," he said. "Is it serious?"

"Only tests. They're doing tests."

"Nutkin", he thought again. I suppose she really does dislike me. He ought to know which school the boy was at.

"Tests?" he said.

"Yes," she said. "It begins with tests, doesn't it?"

Poor Toni

In the fall of the afternoon, when the lights came on in the piazza, Gaetano arrived, and they would play bridge. They did this principally to please Toni's mother, who didn't like being in Rome, but couldn't summon the willpower to return to Venezuela. Or perhaps it was money she lacked, Dallas couldn't be sure. One day it seemed one thing, the next the other. It was that sort of life they were leading.

Toni's mother was Lily-Ann. She would have liked, Toni said, to be addressed as "Miss Lily-Ann", because she had been a Southern belle, and still saw herself that way. She had been spoiled as a girl, Toni said, and had never recovered. It made her a lousy mother. As for Toni, she had been a star of Venezuelan television when she was sixteen, some years back. She had very nice legs, but usually hid them in trousers, and it was some time after he met her that Dallas realised how nice they were. That was one night when Gaetano was playing the piano in the bar where he worked, and Dallas and Toni got drunk and went to bed together. "It's all right if Gaetano doesn't know," she said; but Dallas wasn't sure. He thought it might complicate matters.

Lily-Ann complained a lot in the mornings, as well as in the afternoon when they played bridge. Gaetano was the best player, but she wouldn't admit that. She disapproved of Dallas too, and quarrelled with Toni because she had lost her modelling job, and they didn't know where the money was coming from. In theory there was a monthly cheque from Toni's ex-husband in Munich, but the theory wasn't always translated into practice. When that the cheque didn't turn up, Dallas lent Toni money. Calling it a loan made things more comfortable. It was because of the loans that Lily-Ann tolerated Dallas. Once he suggested he lend her money to buy her air ticket, but it was one of the days she lacked willpower. "There's nothing for me in Venezuela," she said. Dallas thought there was nothing for her in Rome either; but he was wrong there. There was Toni, poor Toni, and Lily-Ann intended to keep a tight hold.

After bridge they went out to eat, leaving Lily-Ann in the apartment because she didn't like Italian food anymore than she liked Italy or Italians. Then they went on to Gaetano's bar. He played a gentle sub-jazz with neat improvisations on popular tunes. Toni sometimes let herself be picked up by men who would buy her whisky rather than Stock, the Italian brandy they usually drank.

She would make them buy whisky for Gaetano and Dallas too. Most times she declined to go off with them, but sometimes she did so.

One night when this happened Dallas got into conversation with a pretty American boy called Erik. He had soft blond hair and a creamy voice, and he complained that men were always trying to pick him up. Dallas said, politely, that he could see why. "I don't like it because I'm not that way," Erik said, moving his face very close to Dallas.

"Well, that's fine," Dallas said. "It doesn't worry me. Nothing does. Have a drink."

Later, when they had had a few drinks, Erik crossed over to the piano, and laid his hand on Gaetano's shoulder and asked him if he could play "La Vie en Rose".

"It's my favourite song," he said, "my very favourite. It says everything."

"You're an old-fashioned boy," Dallas said, and drank some brandy. "The Stock solution to all our problems," he said, reciting the old line, but then called the barman and said he would switch to grappa.

Erik said he was a drama student and sang and danced too. "Just a chorus-boy at heart," Dallas said.

After that, Erik was often in the bar, and always asked Gaetano to play "La Vie en Rose", and would sing it with him. He sang it almost well enough. Toni said he was a bloody little tart, and Dallas smiled. Then one night, when Toni had gone off with an admirer, Gaetano and Erik departed together, and Dallas was left alone with his grappa and the barman. When he went back to his hotel there was a big moon over Monteverde and the air was fresh and good. They were beginning to assemble the market stalls in Campo dei Fiori.

Gaetano picked a quarrel with Toni on account of her departure with the man who had bought her whisky, who was a big Dane called Oskar. So he stopped coming to the apartment to play bridge, and Toni refused to go to his bar. Dallas had said nothing about Gaetano and Erik, though that was why Gaetano had picked the quarrel, and when he still went to the bar himself, Erik was always there, purring like a kitten.

Lily-Ann was displeased about the lack of a fourth for bridge.

"What about Oskar?" Dallas said to Toni, but her reply was brief and obscene. So that was over too, and they recruited an Englishman who wore an Inverness cape and used to arouse the derision of the boys who hung around the piazza and would wolf-whistle as he passed. He pretended not to hear them. "I've always only been able to make love to people of my own class," he confided to Dallas. His bridge was poor, but he talked a lot about "my friend the Cardinal" – though Dallas always wanted to say: "I thought we had more than one of them here in Rome" – and he called Lily-Ann "Miss Lily-Ann", which together, in her view, made up for the quality of his bridge.

Dallas now slept more often with Toni, except on nights when she went to Rosati's in the Piazza del Popolo, which was full of people who hoped to see film-stars or get into movies themselves. Sometimes she said Charles Bronson was there, but of course if she went off with anyone, it was somebody less famous.

That didn't happen too often though, because most of the people at Rosati's were already attached, and because the strain of living with Lily-Ann was having its effect on Toni's looks. Rosati's was expensive, and the requests for a loan from Dallas were becoming more frequent. He continued to oblige because it was easier than saying no. In exchange she suggested he move into the apartment. He managed to say no to that.

"My paper has the hotel number," he said, "and you don't have a telephone."

"You could always arrange to pick up messages," she said; but he let that rest. Altogether he was getting too involved. So he went round to Gaetano's bar to see how things stood.

"No, *caro*," Gaetano said.

"Why not? You know Erik is a little bitch."

"Certainly," Gaetano said. "But, you see, the little bitch is in my system and, to tell you the truth, *caro*, though he is indeed a little bitch, I was glad to have the excuse to leave her. You too, my friend, are now looking for an excuse, isn't that true?"

"Do I need one?"

"Certainly," Gaetano said, "or you will feel bad. You could have had Erik. He would rather have gone with you at first than with me, but not now."

"It's an excuse I'm not sorry to have passed on," Dallas said, and tapped Gaetano on the head, and came away.

He crossed the river and walked through the town he loved as he had loved no other, and up past the Jesuit church and its piazza where the wind always blows waiting for its companion the Devil to emerge from the church, which he never does, and past the Palazzo Venezia where Mussolini used to keep his study light burning to persuade the ever-sceptical Romans that he never ceased from work, and then along the narrow Piazza dei Santi Apostoli and past the Trevi Fountain, till he reached a little bar, by the offices of *Il Messaggero*, which opened at four in the morning. It was a bar where he had more than once got into a fight and he rather wanted to do so now, but there were no takers that morning, and he drank grappa and Peroni chasers till the sky was blue. Then he had breakfast at the English tea-rooms in Piazza di Spagna, ham and poached eggs and Indian tea; and then, checking the time in London, called the news editor of one of the papers for which he wrote and told him the news from Berlin sounded interesting: so why didn't he go there and write something?

"Why not?" said the news editor. "Time you did some work, you lazy sod."

He turned back to the American Express and fixed himself a rail ticket. That was fine then. He went to the Greco for a coffee and started to feel guilty; so went back to Amex and inquired about flights to Venezuela.

"Give me two open tickets," he said. "Make one of them one-way." He handed over his plastic, and this time they checked that the card hadn't been reported stolen, though it was the same girl who had supplied the rail ticket. She looked at him oddly as she completed the transaction, and he asked for an envelope, and went down the street to the central post office, and dispatched the tickets with a note to Toni. Then he collected a bag from his hotel and took a taxi to Stazione Termini.

Only when he was in the train did he wonder, with his experience of the Italian post, whether the tickets would ever find their way across the river to her apartment off Santa Maria in Trastevere; and, if so, whether she and

Lily-Ann would use them or cash them in, so that she, poor Toni, could go on trying her luck at Rosati's. If she did, he hoped she would strike gold. He liked her and had nothing against her, except what she had almost come to the point of demanding from him.

Train Talk

“Oh no,” the girl said, “Brewster’s dead.” She looked up at Lake. “It shatters you, reading it like that in the paper as if it was an ordinary piece of news.”

Her voice drifted into the flat fields they were passing through at a speed and with a smoothness that made them seem like a dull travelogue filling those blank stuffy minutes before the main feature.

“What a marvellous life,” she said, “and now I’ve missed my chance. You know he was one of the few people I’d have liked to meet. I’d have been scared of course.” She stopped and lit a cigarette. The hand that held the lighter shook just a little. “I revered him.”

She was very young and she had written some poems, in short lines with jagged endings. Lake looked at her. It was an accident they were eating breakfast together on this north-bound train. She was very pretty too, with a pale face, a little square-jawed but still neat and cool and vulnerable in its youth, and dark smudgy eyes. He had noticed as she came towards him from the other end of the train that her skirt was short, almost a mini, and showed off nice legs, not showgirl’s legs, but what he classified as nice tennis-playing, bottle-party, bedworthy legs. He smiled to himself as he framed his silent description and was a little ashamed too.

They’d met before, once, at the BBC. Then she’d said achingly silly things, such as he could imagine his daughter mouthing. It was natural they should smile now when they met, by chance, on a train, in travellers’ limbo, and should sit down to have breakfast together. Why, he’d even read some of her poems, found them out in a little magazine. The jagged endings had interrupted anything she was saying before it became too dangerous.

And now she said again, “Brewster’s dead, Brewster.” He nodded.

“Did you ever know him?” she said.

Lake, waiting for his kipper, looked out of the window again to avoid those dark smudgy eyes; puppy’s eyes.

But she persisted.

“You’ll think I’m naive”, she said, “but people like Brewster, not that there are many like him, have real glamour for me.”

“He wrote some good stuff,” Lake said, admiring her defensive irony, the inverted commas she so audibly placed around the words “real glamour”.

We all have those figures, he might have consoled her. Hemingway was one of mine, and I could give you a whole list. Poor old Lowry and Dylan and a host of them. I remember Connolly’s sad moon of a face as I once saw it plain – very plain – in the Ritz Bar; Mailer came in then, and Connolly collected a bottle of champagne, and they retired to a table in one of the pink alcoves. Later, when I knew of his tax problems, I thought of the champagne and hoped the *Sunday Times* paid for it. Oh yes, glamour.

He might have said all that or he might have spoken differently. “You should have been content to remain simply a reader,” he was tempted to say. “That way you could have kept the illusions you are going to find dimming...”

In fact he said, “You remember Auden, don’t you?” He was a bit ashamed again to be talking of Auden while he was waiting for his kipper. “Poetry makes nothing happen...”

It hurt her hearing those words. She was so sure they shouldn’t be true. She only used those timid lines and jagged endings because she didn’t yet really know what the poem was going to make happen; when she found out she would change the world.

“But he was wrong,” she said.

And he almost replied: "People who make things happen don't read. Nobody who makes things happen reads after he is twenty-five. We talk to babies and to other writers, who may therefore actually be babies too. In a certain sense they undoubtedly are. Now I grant you of course that what we say may be true and beautiful and even sublime, but it doesn't matter to anyone except ourselves. I don't think it ever did. It's as significant as making jigsaws. Nobody but a poet ever thought poets were the unacknowledged legislators of mankind. And anyway what's the point of a legislator who isn't acknowledged? Making up laws in a vacuum – it's like Aesop's bullfrog."

Instead he told her that, yes, he had known Brewster. Her lip trembled like a girl opening a love-letter; she looks like a camellia, he thought.

"I can't believe he's dead. Of course for me and for so many others he never will be. ."

"I don't know that he had much liked living for a long time back..." he said.

You can't, he thought, save people pain, not if they have any awareness, and this girl has. The pale spire of a fourteenth-century church rose into view across the fields of beet, a tractor chugged over the mud-grey land towards a Dutch barn under a huge pearly sky. They passed a pond half-choked with weeds, and there was a swan on the little water.

"He was discontented," he couldn't help saying. "I met him when he came back from the States to that Oxford fellowship. He hated Oxford."

"It couldn't ever have been the right place for him," she said. She sounded Edinburgh for the first time as she said this.

"Oh I don't know," he said. "He'd got round to disliking anywhere except hotel rooms. He once said to me, I'm a middle-aged child of the motel revolution. I don't think it meant much, it was just something to say, and he'd said it before. Time and again I shouldn't wonder."

"He was a drinker, wasn't he?" she said, sipping her coffee and not seeming to notice how bad it must be – he had ordered tea himself.

"A good deal of gin. Tumblers of gin and water at all his readings, a tumbler by his bedside, he used to say. He liked to wake in the night and listen to the silence and ease the shadows away with a good swig of the old reliable. Or at least he liked saying that. I must have heard him say that a dozen times."

"You knew him well then?"

"No, not well."

"What did he like, what gave him happiness?"

She had shed two years since they started talking. His kipper arrived. He busied himself separating the flesh from the bone and skin, rather messily.

He liked having people around him and making a fuss of him. He was a lonely man. He liked Westerns and a good cry; Gary Cooper alone in that empty street at high noon. A proud man who was ashamed of being as he was and flaunted what he was. A very frightened man, frightened of the police, frightened of being beaten up, frightened, God help us, of the critics. He had very few interests left when I knew him and was happiest on a bar stool for the two hours before he began to weep. You see, all he had in life was the facility for moving words around on paper, shuffle, shuffle, like a pack of cards, and dealing a poem.

Again of course he hadn't spoken; what was the point? The swan was long out of sight and the landscape was now quite featureless, not even a tree, no human habitation, only a tiny speck in the far distance, another tractor, as it might have been an insect. After all, the girl dealt poems herself.

"There's always a gap between the public life and the private one," he said, "unless you become the mask you have adopted. If you do that, well, you may exist in contentment, but your soul fattens like a pig in a sty. If you don't, if at night you take off the mask with the rest of your make-up, well then, the writer disappears. He is no longer what the reader, who is often anyway only a fan, has imagined. Instead all you have is a person with aches and pains and fears and tax problems. Poor Brewster had terrible tax problems, worse than Connolly's even. He almost had to go to prison once, you know."

Yes, he had actually said that.

"It's monstrous," she replied, "we ought to be like Ireland or Sweden."

He looked out of the window again. The grey shimmered. "Going north," he said. "Going north. How do you feel about going north?"

She looked at him with a faint mist in her eyes like a sea mist. Maybe she was still thinking of Brewster and his fear of buff envelopes; maybe his question had no meaning for her. For himself, going north meant the return to duty and all too often, especially in his youth, the acknowledgement of failure; it was a journey back, a return to the wire perimeter of judgement and obligation. A voyage south on the other hand, the night train to King's Cross or the boarding of an express at the Gare de Lyon which would allow him to wake to Provence or Italy, led always away from himself to a future he could hope to fashion. The South never disappointed; he saw colours only in the South. Brewster of course had sought whatever he was looking for in the West. And that hadn't worked.

"It's like the food in American women's magazines, my dear. That's California; it looks marvellous and tastes of nothing."

So he'd come back also, to Thames Valley fog and then finally to a small hotel in Berlin, where he had died in a bedroom that looked out on the Wall that had marked the inescapable defeat of his sort of Europe. Poor Brewster, child of illusion; like the rest of us, he thought.

Another church, this time abandoned; or rather, he saw now, converted into a shed for machinery. The churchyard which must once have surrounded it, probably not so very long ago, had been ploughed up; and the Church, a mediocre example of Decorated Gothic (to judge from the windows, now empty of glass and boarded up) stood like a rocky outcrop in a sea of sugar beet.

The girl said, "And I was feeling so happy. I've just been seeing my publisher."

The words came in a rush as if she felt she was doing something immodest, boasting of having a publisher of her own.

"There's going to be a book, is there?" he said, keeping a smile back in case she thought it was patronising. And it would have been, though in its way loving too.

"Yes," she said, "in the spring."

"Who's doing it?"

She named a firm he had never heard of.

"Good," he said, "you're happy with them, I hope."

"Oh yes," she said, "they're very enthusiastic. I was lucky with the timing," she said, "I've to be back in school to-morrow."

"School?"

"Yes, I teach, you know. It's my first year of teaching."

It made him sad that she was old enough to be employed, that she had already started on the treadmill; he would have liked her to be even younger than that.

The train, he became aware, had stopped; opposite the church. A skein of geese flew over, heading for the sea.

"What do you make of that?" he said.

She looked, first blankly, then in surprise: "Oh the birds," she said, "nothing really."

"I meant that church," he said. "The church?"

"Yes."

"Nothing particular. Should I? It looks sort of forlorn, I suppose."

"Forlorn?" he said. "Is that a word you could use in a poem?"

"Oh no," she said, "it wouldn't be right. You couldn't use a word like that, could you?"

"No," he said, "I suppose not, and yet, you're right, aren't you, forlorn's just what it is. So why couldn't you use the word?"

She smiled and lit another cigarette. "What is this, a seminar?"

He shook his head. "All the same, if it's what it is but you couldn't use the word, isn't that strange?"

"It's been used too often," she said, "so it's a dead word. Make something new, Pound said that. Brewster whom we've been talking about, that's what he always tried to do. You can't use dead words."

"Even when we're in agreement that it's the right one. The right one in this instance. Forlorn. It's what that church is, forlorn."

And more sentences started in his head, sketching out a whole theory of how religion and God were both dead, taking much of our vocabulary to the grave with them, so that what we were left with was something altogether diminished, a starved imagination, a hollow heart. He saw Brewster in his Berlin hotel bedroom, gazing at the Wall.

He looked at the girl, no longer wanting to make love to her.

"Of course you're quite right," he said. "You couldn't put a word like forlorn in a poem. That earth's been stopped for a long time. And as you say, Brewster knew it very well too."

He signalled to the waiter and asked for his bill. The train began to move, with slow jerks. The church shuddered out of his sight, though for some moments the girl kept her smudged eyes on it as it receded into the past of their journey. She put the cigarette between her soft lips and puffed.

"Forlorn," he said. "It's like the knell of parting day, isn't it? Look at that landscape. It's a long time since any ploughman plodded homeward over those fields. Nowadays he gets into his Cortina. Anyway you'll have to excuse me. I must go and do some work. I've a book to read for review. Deadline, you know. It's been nice seeing you again. Best of luck with the book."

She smiled at him and he read the smile like a lost opportunity; not, he knew, that she'd meant it that way. Instead she took a paperback from her bag as though she had been waiting for him to go. She held it up: a volume of Brewster's Essays.

"I feel a bit sick having chosen this," she said.

"He'd appreciate it, I'm sure," he said.

She lowered her eyes to the printed page and he began his journey back up the swaying train.

In the Bare Lands

"No, you most certainly can't see him."

Giles was accustomed to flat refusals. They didn't faze him.

"I don't want to intrude," he said. "I did write, you know, and I've come a long way."

It was cold on the steps of the seedy-looking house which had certainly seen better days.

The woman – you could imagine from her cheek-bones she had once been beautiful – didn't seem impressed.

"You didn't get a reply, did you?"

Giles nodded.

"I know he's very old," he said. "I would have telephoned but you're not in the book."

"Are you surprised?" she said.

"I'm a perfectly respectable person. I'm not a journalist if that's what you're afraid of."

"I don't care who you are. Can't you see that?"

"I'm afraid it's beginning to rain."

The wind which had been blowing for the last two days was now swirling heavy gouts of rain with it. The house – why had it been built facing north? – lay or, rather, crouched directly in its path. Further up the mountain it might be snowing.

"Couldn't you just let me in to explain myself? It reminds me of trying to sell encyclopaedias, standing here."

He turned up the collar of his Donegal tweed coat.

"That couldn't do any harm, could it, Miss Urquhart? You are Miss Urquhart, aren't you, his daughter, I mean?"

When she didn't reply, he turned for a moment and looked back down the valley. There were meadows a couple of hundred feet below and a sort of byre or bothy standing alone. It was limestone country.

"I've got very respectable credentials," he said, "even a letter of introduction. Mr Atkins said he would write too."

"Henry Atkins?"

"Yes, of course.'

It was the first sign that she might relent and he followed it up, though he knew well that what would really count was his docile dejection – his air of a spaniel that isn't being taken for a promised walk.

"I know there's been a postal strike," he said, "perhaps both our letters got lost that way."

"I don't know what you want," she said. "You can't have sold encyclopaedias."

"Not very successfully, I'm afraid."

There was no point in telling her that he'd never come near to needing to do anything like that; friends' accounts had only established it in his mind as the most pathetic of imaginable holiday jobs.

"Well," she said, "he's out just now."

"In this weather?"

"It's the lambing season."

She pointed to the byre below.

"You can come in and talk to me if you like. I'll give you some tea. It's English."

They entered a narrow hall. There was a heavy oak chest and the walls were painted white. The painting had been done a long time ago.

Miss Urquhart said, "We'll go in here. There are no comfortable rooms in this house. I sometimes think that's why my father chose it."

"The bare lands the surgeon's scalpel," said Giles.

"Oh," she looked at him with surprise, "you do know a little then. I promised you tea. Or would you rather have kirsch? It's local."

"I'd love both. I'm afraid that's very greedy.'

Giles gave her his little-boy smile – he had been brought up by a maiden aunt while his parents were on a tea plantation in Assam. "There is whisky," she said, "but that's his."

She went out through a door at the back of the small room to make the tea. Giles stood by the fire and looked around. It was like a Victorian art photograph – "Cottage in the Hebrides," perhaps. There should be an old woman with a shawl round her head sitting at her spinning-wheel by the fire. The only thing that spoiled the effect was the bookcase which ran along the wall beside the door they had come in by. Giles examined it. There were two shelves of Urquhart's books – poetry, history (damned tendentious history, he could imagine), political philosophy, social studies, six volumes of autobiography – Christ, he hadn't realised he'd written so much, and most of it crap. He pulled one out, not bothering to choose.

"The warder had knowledge of which my fellow-prisoners were ignorant. He knew he was a prisoner more closely confined than they." What bloody arrogant nonsense. He put the book back.

He had a feeling, rare to him, of being out of place. If Judkins thought up anymore of these bright assignments he could bloody well follow them up himself.

He sat down – the chair had a straight back and the seat was too short – and pulled out Simon Lumsden's letter. It was brief and badly typed, the signature barely legible. He supposed it might do, though he, remembering Lumsden's animosity, could read reluctance between the lines.

"Simon Lumsden's the man to go to," Judkins had said.

"Isn't he dead?" – his memory of Lumsden was very vague – his name surely hadn't appeared in the papers for at least a decade.

"No, he lives in Gravesend, but he isn't dead."

It was the nearest approach to a joke Judkins could assemble from his card-index mind.

"And what if he won't see me?"

The whole project was unattractive – he would far rather stay in Venice instead of having to drive into the mountains above Bolzano. It was typical of Judkins to come up with something like this – "We've got the unit there, kill two birds with one stone," he could just hear him say it, even though Judkins was more the type of sentimental moron who would put out a bird table in his suburban garden.

"Lumsden'll see you," he had snickered. "All you need do is go along with a bottle of brandy in one hand and a bottle of Scotch in the other."

"But I thought they quarrelled. Will Lumsden's letter do any good?"

"You can get off your arse and try."

Miss Urquhart came back into the room and set a tray down. She poured two cups of very dark tea.

"Milk and sugar?"

"Both, please."

She handed him the cup and a small glass of kirsch and passed a plate with caraway-seed cake on it.

"It's a little stale, I'm afraid. He's finished with politics. You know that? That's why we live out here. He doesn't even like to talk about them. I don't know when he last wrote to the newspapers."

"Well, he's eighty-five, isn't he?"

"The last visitor we had, some time back in the autumn, didn't realise that. He was still looking for a lead from him. He was a boy from Glasgow University. I'm Edinburgh myself."

"I'd better explain why I've come."

"There's no point in that. I only asked you in because it's pleasant to talk English now and then."

She must have seen surprise on Giles's face.

"He'll only talk Gaelic to me. That shows what he feels."

"I didn't realise..."

"He only learned it in prison, you know. In the second war, not the first."

"I thought," Giles had done his homework, "he belonged to the Lallans school at one time."

"That was before the working-man let him down."

"You sound bitter."

"Bitter? You're quite a wit, aren't you?"

Giles began to feel his resentment deepen.

"I've a letter from Simon Lumsden," he said, handing it over.

"Poor Simon," she replied. She only just glanced at the letter and laid it aside. "How is he?"

It wasn't really a question to be answered.

"We haven't seen him for years. Simon had no ideas, you know. He just wanted a cause to attach himself to. Don't look at me like that, please. What do you imagine I think about when I'm sitting here? What have I to think about? The Workers' Republic of Scotland or the Union of Celtic Commonwealths?"

"I haven't said anything. I thought you said he was finished with politics" – if you call that sort of nonsense politics, he nearly added.

"Precisely."

"Look," said Giles, "I didn't want to come here."

"I used to think I was in love with Simon," she said. "I wanted to be. He did too. Oh well, do you know my fate? I chose the wrong man to save."

She started to try to laugh and then to light a cigarette and then to cry – she stopped frozen between the attitudes.

Giles said, "It's a television programme. My boss thought of calling it 'A Leader in Search of a Party'. It's his notion of Pirandello, half-baked, you know, but that's his style, it needn't be as awful as it sounds..." he was speaking too fast, almost unaware of what he was saying and at any moment the ice would break and she would cry.

But instead the door opened and a very tall old man came in. He walked very erect, no suggestion of a stoop. He was wearing a plaid and looked... Giles had once spent a wet afternoon in Aberdeen and between closing and opening time gone into the Municipal Art Gallery (it was a choice between that and "Sex – Swedish-Style", and though he detested great galleries and would run a mile rather than visit the Uffizi or the Prado, he had in certain moods a weakness for provincial ones) and there seen a Landseer of truly impressive ineptitude entitled "Flood in the Highlands", depicting what he took to be a Laird surrounded by family and retainers with assorted livestock perched on cliffs or struggling in the flood-waters... yes, Urquhart looked exactly like Landseer's conception of a Highland chief. He might even have modelled for the painting, or, more probably, based his conception of himself on it.

He didn't look at Giles but said something in what was presumably Gaelic to his daughter. She replied in the same language. Giles couldn't avoid the impression that hers sounded more fluent, even more natural.

Urquhart's hand disappeared somewhere under his plaid and emerged with a key. He unlocked a heavy deal cabinet, took out a bottle of whisky (Talisker, Giles enviously observed) and poured himself a half-tumbler which he swallowed at one gulp. He made another brief remark to his daughter, filled his glass, replaced the bottle, locked the cabinet and marched out of the room.

"Well?"

"I told you it was pointless."

"What in fact did he say?"

"He told me to tell you to get the hell out of here. That's a paraphrase. It's more vivid in the Gaelic."

"I see."

They could hear footsteps overhead.

"Well, I never really thought anything would..." He tried to think of just what he'd like to do to Judkins. "Do you think I could have another drop of kirsch before I go? It's really rather good."

The footsteps marched up and down like a man pacing his cell.

"He'll live to be a hundred, I know he will," she said, but she filled his glass. "You can buy it in the village below."

Giles drank it quickly and shrugged himself into his overcoat. Or something in a cage.

"Thanks, I will, I certainly will."

He might as well get something out of the trip. Mind you, for the first time he conceded that Judkins had a point. Visually it would be damned good, but, still, if the old loony would only speak Gaelic – well, there were bloody few Gaelic speakers and most of them probably had no TV reception. He'd tell Judkins he'd sent him on a two-hundred-mile round trip to interview a monoglot Gael – that'd puzzle him.

"And give my love to Simon. For what it's worth."

"He won't live to be a hundred, that's for sure. I'm not likely to see him again. He didn't like me much."

"No," she said.

It was sleet that was being blown on a diagonal by the wind now. He got into the hired Fiat, and turned, surprising himself, to say something, he didn't quite know what, something to bring life to her, even perhaps just thank you, but the door was already shut, and he drove down into the valley, the sleet changing to a thin rain as he descended.

What Are You Doing Down There?

"What are you doing down there, Uncle Tom?"

The man lying on the bathroom floor opened his eyes. He saw the lapis-lazuli tiles, the crimson bath-mat and then immediately over him, casting a shadow, the sturdy wide-spread legs.

"Ssh," he said.

"But what are you doing on the floor?"

"I'm stalking."

"What are you stalking?"

Jamie crouched beside his uncle.

"Chinese guerrillas," said Tom Durward, enunciating with difficulty.

Jamie put his mouth close to Tom's ear.

"Where are they?" he was whispering now. "Are they lying in ambush?'

"I'm not sure. Maybe you've frightened them off. Don't make a sound."

Jamie held his breath a long time, almost thirty seconds.

"You've been wounded, Uncle Tom. Are you all right?"

"Ssh, someone's coming."

"It's only Miss de Courcy," said Jamie in a disappointed voice. "Miss de Courcy, Uncle Tom's hunting guerrillas, he's been wounded."

"I heard a crash," said the girl. "Did you fall?"

"It's all right," said Tom Durward. "Jamie, go and make a recce through the flat. See if they're hiding."

The small boy began to wriggle in Red Indian style across the floor that had become a jungle. He moved with concentrated skill. When he reached the door he looked over his shoulder and grinned and gave Tom a thumbs-up signal.

"Don't take any risks now," said Tom. "Remember you're our last hope. The cavalry have all been killed."

"Have you been drinking again?" said Miss de Courcy. She knelt down beside Tom and put her arm round him and heaved him to a sitting position with his back propped against the bidet.

"Hell no, I never fall when I've been drinking."

She looked at him with disfavour. He was a big man with fair hair falling over his brow and she didn't like looking at him lying there like an earthquake disaster victim or a beached whale. He was wearing only a sarong and there was blood over his right eye and he was sweating freely.

She held out her arm showing the dark stain of the sweat where the arm had been pressed against his back.

"You're sweating like you've been drinking. Look."

He became aware that she was dressed in a white linen uniform. "Who the hell are you?" he said.

"Heavens don't you remember? I'd better fix that cut."

She went to the medicine cupboard.

"D'you really not remember? I'm the nurse. Nurse de Courcy."

"You've got an Australian accent."

Without replying she started to swab his wound.

"It's not so bad. Mostly blood. You won't need stitching. Not this time."

She attended to it with impersonal efficiency.

"I'll put on a dressing, it'll be safer with a dressing. You have had an anti-tetanus recently, haven't you?"

Tom tried to struggle to his feet.

"What the hell are you doing here? That's what I'd like to know. I don't need a nurse. If you're an Australian, what are you doing in bloody Switzerland? We are in bloody Switzerland?" His voice rose challengingly. He was articulating more clearly now.

"Of course we're in Switzerland. We're in your apartment in Geneva. Where else would we be?"

He sank back against the bidet.

"How would I know? I thought for a minute we were in bloody Hampstead. Even-bloodier-than-Switzerland Hampstead."

"That's better," said Miss de Courcy, "That'll do."

She looked at him critically. "For an intelligent man you employ a very limited vocabulary."

"I'm conserving it. What makes you think you can insult me anyway, calling me intelligent. Help me up, will you."

He swayed, adjusting his balance.

"Do you know Hampstead, Nurse? No? You're lucky. Sodom and Gomorrah, but it's a terrible place. Full of Liberals. Name the cause, they support it. Queers, Cubans, particularly queer Cubans, Arab hijackers, the Viet Cong, Germaine Greer, the environment. Everything except drunks. They don't like drunks. And why? I'll tell you why. They pollute the environment, that's why. That's what they all say, old Durward polluting the environment again."

"Oh God, you have been drinking. It's no use if…"

"Don't be silly. I wouldn't tell you a secret like that if I'd been drinking. My wife told you to ask that question, didn't she?"

"Of course not, of course she didn't."

Tom Durward walked unsteadily out of the bathroom and across the sitting-room to the window. He felt a cramp coming on in his right calf, a modest persistent cramp, like a nagging tooth, not incapacitating. He looked out of the window. He could just see the lake shining in the sun, the view framed by rooftops and trees; to his left was the high-rising spout of the Jet d'Eau.

"You're quite right," he said, "we are in Geneva. Where's Rosie?"

"Your wife? Do you mean to say you don't remember that even. That she's gone back to London? She went yesterday; she said, she couldn't take anymore. Surely you can't have forgotten?"

Tom Durward felt she was almost pleading with him. He shook his head.

"Back to bloody Hampstead. Back to shoulder moral responsibility for the undeveloped underprivileged. We ought to have a drink on that. Not even one drink, one tiny brandy? Just to celebrate? Have it your way, I'll compromise and have a cigarette. Whose nurse are you anyway, mine or Jamie's?"

"Which of you needs me most?" said Nurse de Courcy, smiling for the first time. She was a pretty girl when she smiled. Her teeth were a little too prominent but she brought her eyes into the smile.

"Not Jamie," said Tom Durward. "You don't need a nurse, do you?" he asked the boy, who had reappeared on the fire-escape. He was brandishing a plastic Thompson gun.

"I drove them off," he replied, ignoring the question, but not offended because he knew Tom was joking. "I think I winged one of them, but I'm not sure because they were moving very fast."

"These Orientals do scurry. Thanks a lot anyway."

"Can I go down to the cafe for an ice cream, Uncle Tom? You get awfully hot chasing guerrillas..."

"Of course. You'll maybe find some money on my dressing table."

"I've got money," said Jamie, "I'm rich."

"Is that all right?" asked Nurse de Courcy. "Going down there on his own, I mean."

She blushed as she said this. Tom realised that she didn't want to seem to be criticising him and wondered whether this was for professional reasons.

"Sure it is. Jamie's tough."

"I'm sorry, I didn't mean... he's a delightful boy. We played Scrabble last night. He's awfully good at Scrabble, for his age I mean."

"He gets his extensive vocabulary from me."

"I'm sorry about that too. I'd no right to..."

"Hell," said Tom Durward, "who gives a damn for rights? We're not in Hampstead."

"I didn't quite get the position clear. When I arrived, I mean. Mrs Durward was in a bit of a state. He's your nephew is he, not hers?"

"His father was my brother. They were killed in a plane crash."

"I'm sorry, I'd no idea."

"For a pretty girl you do an awful lot of apologising. Is there any coffee? Could you be an angel and get me a cup?"

"I guess it's what I'm here for."

Tom Durward gazed out of the window and thought, so she's really gone, she really couldn't take it anymore. Maybe it was Jamie and not me that finished it, you can't look after a small boy by sitting on a committee. No, it was the combination, but me most of all and I don't feel a thing except that it's a lovely day and the sun's shining and there's blossom on the cherry trees.

"How would you like to drive up the mountain?" he said to the nurse when she came back with the cup of coffee. "For lunch, I mean."

"Are you going to be in a fit state to eat lunch?"

"You and Jamie will need to eat. I'll sit and cheer. It's in France. Over the border. We can eat outside, there's a lovely terrace."

"Your wife asked me to try to get you back to work."

"If you think I can't eat lunch, it's a cert I can't work. They have mountain trout and mountain lamb and the best pâté you ever ate and you can see for miles, you can see Mont Blanc. Say yes." He smiled, trying to excavate some of the old charm.

"Well..."

"Work hell. Did you see my last picture?"

"I didn't know you were an actor."

"I'm not, I'm a writer. *Return to the Frontier* – did you see it? It was a stinker, a real lulu. Don't mention work."

"I thought a lulu meant something good."

"Not the way I use the word."

"I'd like to come."

"That's great. Why don't you go and run me a bath and then take Jamie for a walk and we'll drive out."

Miss de Courcy looked a little doubtful.

"It's not a trick of some kind, is it? You're not getting me out of the way so you can have a drink?"

She stood irresolute for a moment when he didn't answer but just lifted his coffee cup in his shaking hands and gave her a crooked smile over the rim, and then she turned into the bathroom and he could hear the water running.

"I've put some Badedas in," she said, "I hope that's how you like it."

"Fine. You'll find Jamie in the café next door, he's probably on his third ice by now. He's an addict."

It was perhaps the friendly irony in his voice that prompted her to say "Isn't he a reason for you to try? To stop drinking, I mean. If you're all he has..."

"Shut up. Just shut up, will you. You're so awfully right, but if you don't mind, shut up."

"About half an hour," she said as he closed the bathroom door.

It was a sunken bath, so Tom Durward was able to get into it quite easily, although he had to place his left hand against the wall to steady himself in case he slipped. He lay back in the steaming water and felt his limbs relax. It was legitimate, sweating in the water. He was pleased to be alone, free of the nurse, because he wasn't really alone. His voices had returned. The old *Voces*. It was wrong to dignify them with the Latin; they always addressed him in the crudest vernacular. He must have passed out very early and slept a long time for them to be back this soon. He wasn't really worried; they were a bore and a nuisance and he wished they would find something new to say, but they were no longer frightening. It was difficult hearing two conversations when he was talking to someone else, though actually the voices were usually muted if he was having a real conversation. He didn't now think they were a sign he was going mad. He knew how to deal with them; four days totally without alcohol would see them off, six or seven if he took the occasional drink. That was all it needed, so it wasn't too bad. Except at night. It was bad at night because they wouldn't let him sleep, they promised him nightmares if he slept, and anyway it was difficult to sleep with their incessant muttering and laughter in his ears. He didn't trust himself with the sleeping pills that could cheat them, not since the incident in New York last year. He couldn't trust himself with pills because he wasn't going to trust Jamie to anyone else. That was why he couldn't tell the nurse about the voices. He had known there was some reason. He was afraid of being given ECT, he admitted that. He had seen Robert Campbell in Rome being driven really mad by electric-shock treatment so that he had eventually put his head in a gas oven. There was irony there, he'd never noticed it before, to gas yourself because of electricity.

"Balls, Durward," said a voice, speaking very clearly, "Durward's shit-scared."

If he couldn't trust himself with pills because of Jamie, he wasn't going to trust himself to ECT. But it was bad at night and it was really heroic to endure it and not take pills.

"Durward thinks he's a hero," said a second voice.

"Durward a hero," said the first, "that's a joke, that's a real joke, he's shit-scared. Everyone knows that. Shit-scared Durward."

The voice began to chant it; others joined in.

"Shut up," said Tom Durward.

Instead of pills he made up lists. That sometimes worked. It kept his mind occupied. He always began with Napoleon's marshals. He started with old Kellermann and the three other non-fighting ones and went on to Berthier and Murat and the seven Corps commanders of the *Grande Armée* of 1805 and Masséna; he was always puzzled because he couldn't recall why Masséna, who with Davout was the only marshal who really understood Napoleonic warfare, had been out of favour in 1805 and had not been given a Corps. He always meant to look it up and always forgot. After that there was no fixed order though he tried to keep Grouchy for number twenty-six, not so much because he had been the last appointed as because he held him responsible for the defeat at Waterloo. He always forgot one or two but they were never the same ones. The voices didn't seem to mind this game, perhaps it was just that they were inured to it. They were even ready to suggest names that he might have forgotten, particularly Oudinot, for whom they apparently had a considerable admiration; he didn't know why they had this feeling for Oudinot unless it was that he had suffered thirty-four wounds and yet lived to be eighty-one.

On the other hand the voices deeply disliked and attempted to disrupt the next game, which was to make a list of all those who had opened the England innings with Len Hutton. This was a more difficult task since, while he knew that there were twenty-six marshals, he couldn't remember how many partners the great man had had and so was never certain when he had succeeded. He was doubtful about the South African tour of 1938–9, though he usually settled for Bill Edrich and he had a nagging suspicion that Laurie Fishlock might have opened in one Test against Australia on Hammond's tour; he generally concluded that he had gone in down the order despite being an opening bat for Surrey. If he thought he had completed this list, he went on to catalogue the legion who had opened the England innings after Len's retirement, and this sometimes so disgusted the voices that they retreated and allowed him to doze; this never happened till the third night.

Tom Durward climbed out of the bath with nervous difficulty and shaved. He only nicked himself once and smiled as he tremulously jabbed the styptic at his chin.

"You son of a bitch," he said to his reflection in the glass, "you're going to win through again. Do you think Rosie's gone for good?"

"Of course she has. She can't stand you," said a voice. "Nobody can. They all hate you. Jamie hates you, Durward."

"That's not true."

"You know it's true. He hates you. He'll leave you. That girl hates you. She hates and despises you. It's no use you undressing her, we heard you undressing her, don't try to deny it, we heard you. We're your only friends, Durward, we can't leave you. Poor us, tied to Durward, part of Durward."

"Oh shut up, you talk a lot of bloody nonsense."

"He's talking to us again, that's a very good sign, it shows we've got him. You're going to die, Durward, but that won't get rid of us, he's talking to us again, that's a very good sign..."

The voices began to crow in triumph. Tom dabbed some aftershave on ("Poove," screamed the voices) and went through to his dressing-room. He took the bottle of vodka from its hiding-place and put it on the chest of drawers. I'm not going to drink it, he said to himself, I'm just going to look at it, it's nice to know I can just look at it. He put on a pair of underpants and sat on the couch and tried to ease his socks on. He found it hard going because of the shooting pains in his feet and ankles and when he had managed it he was covered in sweat again. He took the towel and rubbed himself down and looked at the vodka, stared at the vodka but still didn't advance his hand to it, ignoring the odds that the voices were calling. He found a navy-blue towelling shirt that would absorb the sweat and a pair of slacks of the same colour and put them on and slipped his feet, with circumspection to avoid cramp, into a pair of casual shoes without laces. It was all a difficult operation but he had made it without touching the vodka and he could hear that the odds were lengthening; you could get three to one against now. He looked at the array of his ties and scarves and this made him think of Simon Field, who always wore his Old Etonian tie after a particularly heavy or disastrous bat, and how he understood why, though Simon had never noticed this habit of his until Tom pointed it out; but Tom wasn't an Etonian and neither liked nor possessed his own Old School tie and was anyway wearing this towelled shirt. So he selected an Indian silk scarf and wrapped it round his neck; as he did so, he heard the door open and voices which were less distinct than those he had been listening to. He put the vodka back in the false copy of the *Biographia Literaria* which he had had specially made, though he was never sure that Coleridge would have appreciated the compliment, and picked up a cream- coloured linen jacket and went to join them.

"Brilliant timing," he said. "Thank you for looking after him."

"You don't look so bad, in fact you look terrific," Miss de Courcy said, her brow clearing.

Tom realised that she had been afraid that she would find him crouched over a bottle or stretched senseless on the carpet or something and felt glad he had entrusted the hooch to Samuel T.

"Fine," he said, "you go and take that uniform off and we're ready to go."

"Uncle Tom," cried Jamie, shaking his arm to attract his attention, "Uncle Tom, I saw the man with the eye-patch."

"What was he up to?"

Jamie cast a conspiratorial glance round the room and lowered his voice.

"He was pretending to read a newspaper."

"That's pretty sinister," said Tom Durward. "How could you tell he was pretending?"

Jamie thought for a moment.

"His eye was moving the wrong way. Is he really a Tong?"

"There's no doubt about it. He's in league with the guerrillas."

"If he's a Tong, why isn't he Chinese too?"

"He's a double agent."

"A double agent," Jamie repeated. Then he began to giggle. "But don't you see, that makes him a pair of Tongs."

"My God, I hadn't thought of that," said Tom, but Jamie didn't hear. He had collapsed helpless on the sofa.

The car was in the courtyard at the back. Tom Durward was sweating again by the time they reached it.

"This bloody sun," he said, knowing that he deceived nobody. "I hope you can drive."

He gave her the keys. She looked doubtfully at the Bentley. "I don't know that I can drive that."

"Of course you can. All you do is twiddle a few knobs and hold the wheel. Jamie will sit between us and tell you what to do. I don't even know your name, I can't call you Nurse."

"It's Jill, Jill de Courcy."

"Well, what are we waiting for?"

I should have taken that drink, he was thinking, just the one quick necessary therapeutic utterly consular drink. He was tempted to make an excuse, say he had forgotten his money and go back, but he saw the girl giving him a cool appraising look like a tennis-player sizing up her opponent at the start of the final set, and Jamie was in the car already anxious to be off, and he pictured the lift in which he always expected to have a heart attack and got into the car.

As they reached the suburbs he began to sing; Jamie enjoyed this and he had long ago discovered that it kept the voices at bay. He sang "Auprès de ma blonde" and broke into the Marseillaise as they passed the Customs Post.

"Are we going to Madame Papelar's?" asked Jamie.

"Yes."

"She promised she'd let me try on her wig. Do you think she will?"

"She'll keep her promise."

"I like Madame Papelar. I would really prefer to try on her red one, but she keeps that for weddings and Sundays."

They drove out of the houses and through the orchards and up into the vineyards. Tom sang "Sailing up the Clyde" and all the Will Fyffe songs, and first Jamie and then Miss de Courcy joined in the choruses. They were in a holiday mood by the time they arrived at the restaurant and Tom's voices were silent. Gaston, the waiter, gave them a table under the trellis with a view over the valley.

"That's Mont Blanc," said Tom Durward.

Gaston took Jamie by the hand and led him through to the kitchen. “Remember I want wine, Uncle Tom,” he called as he left, “white wine. I like white wine at lunch. Red wine makes you sleepy in the afternoon,” he explained politely to Jill.

“Do you really let him drink wine?”

“Why not?”

“He’s so young. Besides, I would have thought...”

“You would have thought? Oh, I see. Tell me, am I your first alcoholic case?”

Miss de Courcy flushed.

“Well, I have to admit you are.”

“Let me tell you something then. Drink doesn’t destroy people. They destroy themselves. It’s a means, not a cause.”

“Where’s he gone off to?”

“I imagine he’s choosing his trout. If you want to eat trout you’d better go and choose yours. They’ve a tank at the back.”

“Do you mean they’re swimming about and you pick one out and they cook it? Just like that?”

“That’s right. They taste better that way.”

“But it’s horrible. That little thing choosing a trout and having it killed for him. How can you allow it?”

“If you’re going to eat flesh, you’re taking the responsibility of killing. You’ve got to accept that. You’re eating something that’s been alive. It’s one of the things wrong with the modern world.”

“What is?”

“Frozen chickens wrapped up in polythene so that they appear to have no connection with anything that’s been alive. It’s an evasion of responsibility. If you think I should encourage Jamie to dodge responsibility, you’ve an odd idea of the morality involved in bringing up a child.”

“You’re a strange man,” she said.

"In what way?"

"I don't know."

"Alcoholics are people too."

"Monsieur Tom," said Madame Papelar, coming on to the terrace, "it's good to see you."

"And you," said Tom Durward.

"The little one has chosen his fish. He has an eye for a fish."

"What are you going to eat?" he said to Jill.

"You said the pâté was good. I'll have that and a trout too."

For me, simply a smoked trout. You have one with a strong flavour? And some white wine. Half a litre? And a bottle of beer. Very cold, please."

He saw the reproach in Nurse de Courcy's eyes.

"Onc bottle of beer," he said. He held out his trembling hand. "I've got to get so as I can hold my fork," he said, trying to coax a smile. "Hell, one beer can't... French beer. Are you going to choose your fish?"

She hesitated a long minute and got up. She bestowed a reluctant smile on Tom Durward and left the terrace. She walked like an athlete. He lit a cigarette and closed his eyes.

Bessières, Victor, Saint-Cyr...

"Uncle Tom, don't go to sleep. Gaston says there's a party of Japanese have booked a table. That's pretty sinister, isn't it?"

Other titles by Vagabond Voices

www.vagabondvoices.co.uk

Allan Massie's ***Surviving***

About the book

Surviving is set in contemporary Rome. The main characters, Belinda, Kate (an author who specialises in studies of the criminal mind, and Tom Durward (a scriptwriter), attend an English-speaking group of Alcoholics Anonymous. All have pasts to cause embarrassment or shame. Tom sees no future for himself and still gets nervous "come Martini time". Belinda embarks on a love-affair that cannot last. Kate ventures onto more dangerous ground by inviting her latest case-study, a young Londoner acquitted of a racist murder, to stay with her.

Allan Massie dissects this group of ex-pats in order to say something about our inability to know, still less to understand, the actions of our fellow human beings, even when relationships are so intense. It is also, therefore, impossible or at least difficult to make informed moral judgements of others. This is an intelligent book that examines human nature with a deft and light touch.

Comments

"Massie is one of the best Scottish writers of his generation. *Surviving* – sympathetic, unsentimental, atmospheric – is an overdue reminder of how good he is." – Alan Taylor, *The Herald*

"… an impressive novel which poses moral and philosophical questions but works equally well as a compelling thriller." – Joe Farrell, *TLS*

"… an excellent little novel." – Ben Jeffery, *The Guardian*

"The dark brilliance of Massie's style … *Surviving* may be an instant classic in the alcoholic literary canon." – Patrick Skene Catling, *The Spectator*

Price: £10.00 ISBN: 978-0-9560560-2-3 pp. 224

Vagabond Three Vagabond Three Vag

www.vagabondvoices.co.uk

Allan Cameron's ***In Praise of the Garrulous***

About the book

This first work of non-fiction by the author of *The Golden Menagerie* and *The Berlusconi Bonus*, has an accessible and conversational tone, which perhaps disguises its enormous ambition. The writer examines the history of language and how it has been affected by technology, primarily writing and printing. This leads to some important questions concerning the "ecology" of language, and how any degradation it suffers might affect "not only our competence in organising ourselves socially and politically, but also our inner selves."

Comments

"A deeply reflective, extraordinarily wide-ranging meditation on the nature of language, infused in its every phrase by a passionate humanism" – Terry Eagleton

"This is a brilliant tour de force, in space and in time, into the origins of language, speech and the word. … Such a journey into the world of the word needs an articulate and eloquent guide: Allan Cameron is both and much more than that." – Ilan Pappé

I like *In Praise of the Garrulous* very much indeed, not only because it says a good many interesting and true things, but because of its *tone* and style. Its combination of personal passion, observation, stories, poetic bits and serious expert argument, expressed as it is in the prose of an intelligent conversation: all this is ideal for holding and persuading intelligent but non-expert readers. In my opinion he has done nothing better." – Eric Hobsbawm.

Price: £8.00   ISBN: 978-0-9560560-0-9   pp. 184

www.vagabondvoices.co.uk

Alessandro Barbero's ***The Anonymous Novel***

About the book

Set in Gorbachev's Russia, this complex but highly readable novel not only provides a portrait of a society in transition, but also fascinating studies of various themes including the nature of history and the Russian novel itself. Barbero uses his skills as a historian to study the reality of Russian society through its newspapers and journals, and his skills as a novelist to weave a complex plot – a tale of two cities: Moscow and Baku. And throughout, the narrative voice – perhaps the greatest protagonist of them all – represents not the author's views but those of the Russian public as they emerged from one dismal reality and hurtled unknowingly towards another.

Comments

"In the depiction of these changing times, Barbero's political intelligence is apparent. So, however, is his skill as a novelist, for he contrives to integrate the socio-political analysis in his story of imagined characters. It never obtrudes itself; yet you can't ignore or forget it... If you have any feeling for Russia or the art of the novel, read this one. You will find it an enriching experience." – *The Scotsman*

"He writes in a bright and breezy, satirical style ... which leads the reader to believe that some Russian master has been leaning over his shoulder, guiding his hand... It is a deeply rewarding pleasure to be lost in this novel." – *The Herald*

"Barbero uses the diabolic skills of an erudite and professional narrator to seek out massacres of the distant and recent past. *The Anonymous Novel* concerns the past-that-never-passes (whether Tsarist or Stalinist) and the future that in 1988 was impending and has now arrived." – *Il Giornale*

Price: £14.50 ISBN: 978-0-9560560-4-7 pp. 464